The Roan Maverick

To order additional copies, please contact us.
BookSurge, LLC
www.booksurge.com
1-866-308-6235
orders@booksurge.com

C R STRAHAN

THE ROAN MAVERICK

2006

East Baton Rouge Parish Library
Baton Rouge, Louisiana

The Roan Maverick

For Tom Tisdale
And All Those Cowboys Of The Open Range Who Gave
Me A Story To Write—
You Own The Brand On The Roan Maverick, Fellas!

PROLOGUE
Red Fork of Powder River, 1967

It has been said that time heals all wounds. Perhaps that is because the passions life tend to dim with age, some mellowing as wisdom comes, some simply fading away along with youth and vitality. Many of my own wounds have withered to a mere memory, like distant youth, though I am still waiting for time to do its work on the deepest of them. As a young woman, I watched in fascinated terror as moneyed arrogance became tyranny, tyranny spawned rebellion, and the resulting range war marched up my porch steps and barged through the door.

I am old as a relic now—age has become a curious ally. Death has stalked me for a century without hitting its mark. I have sidestepped accidents, war, and epidemics to outlive them all—my husband, my children, my friends, even my enemies. I have seen this nation go from the covered wagon to the jet airplane, and even lived to hear its president vow to put a man on the moon before the decade ends. It would be a magnificent feat, to be sure. But it seems an odd thing to contemplate from the porch of this old homestead. In the silence of this red-walled valley, shaped by eternal wind and water, to imagine that a man may soon tread on that old Hunter's Moon in the sky only makes me shake my head in wonder—and resignation.

Men simply cannot resist a new frontier.

My husband was no exception. He was a Texan, born and raised, and to his way of thinking Texas by 1880 was too settled to be considered a frontier any longer. So he came north with the trail herds that were destined for Powder River and its vast stretches of untouched grass.

We met in Montana, where I had lived since the age of four—my parents having chosen the Rocky Mountain West as their place of exile from Virginia after the War of the Rebellion. Having come west so young and been raised on the frontier, I had no concept that Montana was a meager outpost of civilization—it was simply home to me. And, Lord!—how I wish Jack and I had stayed there after we met and courted. But we didn't. We started our married life in Dakota and later moved to Wyoming, following the opportunities afforded by America's red-hot love affair with the cattle business. History calls that era the great Beef Bonanza. I have other names for it, but we'll stick to the historical handle for the time being.

It is difficult for me to tell this tale.

If only grass could talk, Powder River's country itself might tell the story of Wyoming's Cattle War. And I mean the *real* story—not the narrow political and economic records of the history books. And not some Hollywood shoot-'em-up that's all heroes and villains, either. And certainly not the propaganda generated by wealthy cattlemen to conceal the lethal nature of their arrogance. This grassland would tell the story in wide-open reality, unencumbered by emotion, prejudice, or the numbers on a balance sheet.

At its best it is a tale of ordinary people lured by nature and opportunity, many of whom became extraordinary when assaulted by sudden injustice. At its worst it's a stark tale of infamy spawned by the usual infamous suspects—betrayal and greed, violence and murder. The most human element of this story's reality is that the heroes didn't all line up on one side and the villains on the other. I like to think that our side had a monopoly on the heroes, but I'm not fool enough to pretend the villains were all theirs. I'd like to hear what this grassland might say about that.

But so far the grass hasn't spoken, and neither had those ordinary people before they passed on. Since I'm the only one left who lived through it, I suppose the job of telling the tale has finally been left at my door. There was a time when I vowed never to speak of it again, and I have kept that vow for nigh onto eighty years. Only one person in this world could possibly convince me that this story *needs* to be told, and she's sitting here in front of me. Waiting patiently. She's not one to ask for frivolities—she reminds me of myself at her age, which was the very era we moved to this valley of Red Fork.

We came here in 1887, my husband Jack and I. Martin, the oldest of our four children, was just a baby then, and the other three weren't even gleams in our eyes yet. I didn't want to come. I liked our life on the Dakota plains. Jack had a good job there managing the ranch of a wealthy easterner. We had a nice house with more fixtures than a prairie home should wish for, a prolific garden, a larder brimming with staples, and stimulating conversations with the owner when he was out from New York. He was a robust young man and enjoyed the climate and the frontier immensely.

I can admit now that it was mostly vanity that made me want to stay in Dakota. Beyond coveting the house and the foodstuffs, I was an educated woman—a rarity in those days—and I felt the world owed me those stimulating conversations. Our employer was particularly fond of my headstrong wit. He was a Harvard man with graduate studies in law at Columbia, and even a stint in the New York legislature under his young belt. Every visit he brought the current eastern newspapers and some glorious treasure we plains dwellers could never seem to find on the frontier. Silk thread, books, a bolt of Irish linen. I still have the highchair he gave us at Martin's christening, and the photograph he took of me in sidesaddle on my favorite horse.

I enjoyed that man probably more than I should have. He was bursting with life, owned a keen intellect and a remarkable appreciation of the natural world—a characteristic not often inherent in men of wealth and renown. He made our time in Dakota a worthy joy. We were both equally fond of him, though I sensed a burgeoning uneasiness on Jack's part after our employer, Mr. Roosevelt, lost his beloved wife.

It wasn't jealousy, for Jack was the picture of self-assurance and could hold his own with any man. Perhaps it was the knowledge that *this* man was truly his equal and exactly the sort of eastern gentleman my mother had wanted me to marry. Even though young Mr. Roosevelt went on to international acclaim at the helm of our nation and led a life of progressive service unequalled by his peers, I wouldn't say he was *more* than Jack's equal. In his day my husband engineered a movement of rebellion against tyranny, and his legacy of invoking the power of justice lives on here in Wyoming as surely as the legacy of Theodore Roosevelt lives on within the nation.

Our few short years on the Dakota plain were the happiest of my life. Though I have grown to love this mountain valley, with its red sandstone walls and abundant grass, far more than I could ever have loved the wide Dakota plain, I would go back to Dakota and start it all over if I could. I would endeavor to be even more headstrong, though less vain and obsessive. Every life surely has its regrets. But we could never have known the trouble that lay ahead when we came here. I have told myself time and again that no one should be made to endure what I have endured. And it's true. But I also limited that truth to an excuse for my obsessions, and some of them proved damaging to my children.

No excuse can justify that.

The wind sings to me now in the cottonwoods and willows along the river, echoing off the high wall to the west. I still mourn the loss of my loved ones, Jack most of all. He was taken too soon, torn from our lives by the arrogant rudeness of fate.

Sing to me, Jack. Come back on this wind; sway me gently. I have known too little gentleness since you left. This country made me hard and unforgiving—I was lonely and stunted after your death.

And I have missed you for too long.

CHAPTER ONE
WEST FROM DAKOTA

(Excerpt from the journal of Josie Watson Stewart)

September 17, 1887 - Nearing our destination. This country has a stronger roll to it than Dakota, like storm swells at high sea. I have never seen such grass. A year ago it was non-existent, dried to dust from the most severe drought the forks of Powder River have known. But the winter that followed was a horror beyond description, the worst ever recorded. Cattle died here in untold thousands, sending all but a handful of the big stock outfits that graze their cattle hereabouts into receivership. A pall of tangible and economic death lies over this magnificent rangeland. The moisture came too late and far too furiously to rescue the cattlemen's empire from ruin. It seems a sad irony that the winter, which killed the cattle, also brought the new grass growth that would have sustained them. In spite of it all, and in spite of my many misgivings in leaving Dakota, it is a truly splendid country. The spirits are alive here—not merely the spirits of the dead cattle, but those of the buffalo who came before. This was sacred ground to the Crows, because the buffalo fattened on the rich grasses year round— even in winter! It is truly beautiful country. The mountains are its crowning joy; I have been watching them for days in anticipation. Our homestead lies there in a valley along the foothills just ahead. I will be glad to finally step down from the wagon in a place above and beyond this seemingly endless sea of grass. I have felt at times like a shipwreck victim adrift in a forever sort of distance, anchored only by those far-off mountains and the occasional withered and smelly abomination of cattle carcasses. Remnants of the killer winter, these innumerable corpses are a nasty surprise within the grass. The final infamous storm of the winter lasted an unfathomable fifty-four days. To add insult to injury, it was followed by Chinook winds that melted the snow in a deluge, filling all the watersheds with raging torrents and rotting carcasses. The sheer beauty of the mountains and abundance of new range growth are all that outweigh the ominous presence of death. It's a haunting scene.

September 18, 1887 - We have arrived! Our valley is more glorious than I could ever have imagined. I have begged Jack's forgiveness for all my reluctance in moving here. This place is wonderful, protected from the elements, alive with subtle colors beyond description. Trees, grass, abundant water, red cliffs, and granite. Our cabin sits along the river in the trees. It is nicer than the other two we passed downstream, both inhabited by several cowboys, most of whom are Jack's boyhood friends from Texas. His brother Allison lives alone on adjacent filing in a lean-to as rough and unsavory-looking as he himself. But I should not think in such uncharitable terms. It was, after all, these lonesome cowhands who built the cabin for us. For me, really. Allison, rawboned recluse though he appears, wanted me to step down from that dusty, jolting wagon into a home. It's no small thing that these men have done for us, and I am truly grateful. I just wish they had thought to bathe before greeting us.

It seems my vanity knew no bounds in those days. Expecting such hardworking range men to interrupt their lives and bathe for my benefit rings with haughty conceit. I admit it. I was a frontier elitist—a snob, holding myself above those *uneducated* men. It wasn't as though they were illiterate. They could all read, write, and cipher. One of them, a West Virginia man, had even acquired some higher education. He later taught school in the valley when there were enough children to form a school district, and went on to become quite an accomplished writer in his middle years.

But at the time they all looked the same to me, dressed in a month's worth of dirt, shy smiles, neglected stubble and dusty moustaches, hats in their hands. To a man, they all sported that hallmark of the range hand—a crescent of white forehead at the top of the brow. They greeted Jack with ear-wide grins, boisterous handshakes, and uninhibited hugs.

"Jack, you know everybody here except our new pardner, John Burgee," said Allison. "He comes outta West Virginia."

Burgee offered his hand.

"Please to meet you," Jack smiled. "And fellas, this is the light of my life, my lovely Josie."

They fawned over me adoringly, even though they were intimidated by gender—and demeanor. I wore my education and class like some holy birthright. They wouldn't allow me to unload one item from that wagon, but ushered me to the comfort of a rocking chair on the porch, where I sat with baby Mart as they moved us in.

"Don't get up, Miss Josie," they said, hefting boxes and furniture up the steps. "Just point us in the right direction."

They had truly outdone themselves in building the cabin. It was made of logs and was quite large and well-appointed for a homestead of the era—four rooms, real glass windows, cupboards and closets, and that delightful south-facing porch. The rocking chair was my house-warming gift from Allison.

I didn't even have to cook a meal in return for all that work— they wouldn't hear of it. Whit Fielder graciously chased me out of the kitchen and prepared an elk stew for the crowd while Jack and I looked over our new place.

"What do you think, darlin'?" he said as we strolled along the river. "Ally picked us a good spot, didn't he?"

"It's absolutely beautiful, Jack. I don't know if I've ever seen a lovelier valley. And the house is wonderful—far more than I expected."

He grinned. "Didn't think a bunch of tough range-ridin' bachelors could build a house for a woman, did you?"

"I had some doubts," I admitted.

"Allison knows good cattle and land, but he's too much a lonesome rangehand to know anything about a lady's home. So I wrote to Will Standifer and told him what I wanted. Sent him some money."

It wasn't as pretty as the house in Dakota, but it was all ours.

I marveled at the size of the kitchen and wondered if Jack had been less than candid when he said three or four children would suit him just fine—this kitchen was big enough to accommodate a column of cavalry. But later that evening I began to discern his intended design as all the men lounged comfortably around our oak table to renew their friendship with stories and liquid refreshment. I had retired to the bed chamber, but I listened, fascinated at their easy camaraderie.

"Sure is good to see you, Jack," said Will Standifer, and the others concurred.

"It's good to be here, fellas."

"Well, Jack, now that you're here, maybe you can help us learn how to keep up with your little brother," said Billy Shaw, and they all laughed.

"The man who tries to keep up with Allison," Jack said, "is gonna grow old fast. You all should know that."

"Don't we, though," said Whit. "The other day we were all out on Burro Flat and we stumbled on a five-year-old steer—biggest slick you ever seen. I doubt the crittur'd ever spied a human in all its surly life. He was eyein' us and shakin' his horns like he was ready to have us all for breakfast. While we sat there marvelin' at his size, Ally just rides out there, ropes him and ties him down without so much as a by-your-leave. Shamed us silly."

"Whit, I don't recall you being awed by such work," Jack remarked. "Every one of you boys does the same thing day-in-day-out."

"Not on raw horses, we don't," said Billy.

Will nodded. "If it'd been anybody but Allison, they'd've been jerked down by that maverick for sure—Whit ain't just whistlin' Dixie about the size of that steer."

"How raw was your horse, Ally?" asked Jack.

"'Bout like that side of elk hangin' in the pantry."

"You'd never roped on him before?"

Allison shrugged. "Can't teach a horse to rope without showing him how at least once."

4

"And you know Ally," added Whit, "he's gotta find the biggest, ugliest steer on the range to teach this poor dumb horse to rope with."

Allison grinned. "We was just tryin' to keep you boys on your toes."

They all laughed again.

"Well, I'm not surprised," said Jack. "Ever since he was a kid, Ally could rope anything on anything. He's probably got more horse savvy in his little finger than the group of us does all around."

"It was a foolhardy stunt, if you ask me," said Burgee.

"That's probably why we didn't ask you, John," said Ben Lattis, and they all laughed again—except Burgee.

"Well, Ally's had plenty of practice ropin' big mavericks lately," said Whit. "Besides tryin' to out-rustle every Association outfit in Wyoming, he's had to gather a herd for you, Jack."

This time everyone laughed but Jack. I'm not sure anyone in that room caught the pause between Jack and Allison, but I did— and I was two rooms away.

They talked late into the night and still had the energy to get up and cook breakfast for me. How paradoxical that these tough range professionals, who bowed to no man and harbored a good-natured though active contempt for money and social position, would defer so willingly to me.

In retrospect, I must attribute my misperception of what motivated their behavior to my own vanity. In truth, it was Jack to whom they were bowing in deference. I was only a part of his aura, the glint on his halo, but I was too self-absorbed to recognize it then. They *loved* him. He was their boyhood chum made good.

The majority of them had grown up together as ranch children in Texas, riding, roping, and handling stock. But Jack had gotten himself an education—and not anything sissified, either; something they could all respect. He had studied the law and graduated with honors from St. John's College.

I do not mean to insinuate that cowboys naturally respected law degrees or people who attended venerated colleges. On the contrary, higher education in general and lawyers in particular were by and large held in cowboy contempt—it was a well-known truth among range hands that lawyers only got you out of the kind of trouble you'd never get into if there weren't any lawyers. But Jack's case was different to them, you see. It wasn't just that he had been a cowboy before his father's Texas Masons had provided the scholarship that sent him to college; it was that—to their way of thinking—he had had the good sense to become a cowboy again afterward.

The truth of the matter was, Jack found indoor work deplorable. He had attempted to put his degree to good use by taking an apprenticeship with a lawyer in Austin, but after a year he found he could not reconcile himself to a life lived indoors. So he came north with the trail herds, as many young men did in those days.

I met him in Mingusville, Montana. I had recently returned there from my stint at a finishing school in the east to help my mother run her boarding house. Mingusville, later renamed Wibaux, was a railhead and quite the bustling frontier town. Mother had spent a good deal of the money my father had left us on my education. With what remained she built the boarding house and prepared to see herself through widowhood. Mother was a refined Southern gentlewoman, and the prospect of engaging in commerce ran contrary to all of her upbringing. But she had come of age during the War of the Rebellion, and had learned to disregard childhood teachings that no longer applied.

My father had been a medical doctor. He was pressed into the service of the Confederacy as a surgeon, though he despised the institution of slavery and rightly predicted that it would be the South's undoing. I was born in Richmond, but I was too small to remember much of the War, except the noise of the cannons when Richmond fell.

When the War ended, my parents migrated to the frontier to build a new life. I wonder that they didn't choose someplace warmer—the Southwest perhaps, or California; father never could acclimate himself to winters on the northern plains. He had bronchitis every January, the cases worsening each year. Pneumonia eventually took him when I was fifteen. Shortly thereafter, Mother packed me off to finishing school in Delaware.

She didn't want me to come back west.

"You're an attractive young lady, Josephine," she told me, "and it's my fervent hope that you will meet and marry an intelligent eastern gentleman and go on to live a more refined, less strenuous life. Montana is rough country, especially for women."

"But *you're* here, Mama. If you feel that way about Montana, why would you want to stay?"

Her smile betrayed only the barest hint of the scars left by the war. "Everything I knew, everyone I loved back there no longer exists. *This* is where your father died. This is where I belong."

I understood what she was saying, but I couldn't desert my only-known relative for what I viewed as a foreign country. Every Western child grows up knowing that strangers are more so east of the Mississippi. And the West was home to me. I could never appreciate the East enough to live there, cluttered and close on city streets that smelled of decay and neglected horse dung. The West may have been crude and short on amenities, but there was openness and clear air, blue skies. And somehow the smell of horse dung was never offensive to me along the upper Missouri—must have been all those range-fed horses.

The boarding house was doing a booming trade by the time I returned. It wasn't anything fancy: a rough, three-story log affair that sounds bigger than it was. The main floor was mostly kitchen and dining area. The second story had six boarding rooms, and the third floor wasn't more than an attic, where our oldest feather mattresses were lined out like slabs in a city morgue—it was the boarding house equivalent of the cheap seats at the theater. Any man who didn't want to pay for more than a place to throw down his bedroll could do so there for twenty-five cents a night. To cowboys it was a first-rate paradise. Mother and I referred to it euphemistically as Heaven. What a chore it was to keep that room free of vermin! All told, though, it was the space that brought in the most money. The first time I met Jack he had taken lodging there.

That was sort of a funny night, now that I remember it.

Late that afternoon Jack had brought in his employer's cattle for market shipment. With him were his brother Allison and their wrangler, a youngster of about fourteen years. With his trail pay, the boy had bought himself a pocketful of cigars and allowed Allison to treat him to a beer. He was feeling pretty jovial as they all walked back along the holding pens checking their stock. And as they came upon a disgruntled-looking railroad worker, the boy attempted to brighten the man's disposition by offering him a cigar. He got pushed in the mud for his trouble. I suppose I should mention that there was never any love lost between railroaders and cowboys.

As Allison helped the boy to his feet, Jack stepped up to the man and entreated him to apologize. The man refused.

"I beg your pardon, sir," Jack said respectfully, "but this young man offered you a cigar out of kindness—a neighborly gesture—and apology is the only reasonable response that could suit this situation."

Jack was very bright and had the gift of diplomacy. His position as a range boss required him to wear a revolver, but he had no intention of using it—even on a man as obstreperous as the railroader.

Allison was a different story. He also carried a pistol, which he proceeded to pull forthwith. "You can apologize, or you can dance, mister," he said.

"Or I can spit in your eye, you stinking saddle tramp! Go to hell!"

I doubt Allison even knew how to spell diplomacy. He commenced firing at the railroader's feet until he was satisfied that enough dance steps had been taken to compensate for the shove in the mud, then walked on with the youngster.

This, of course, ignited the railroader's peeve into a perfect rage. It seems he had been accosted that morning by a group of cowboys and had mistaken Jack's group for the perpetrators. Hence the shove in the mud. The dance lesson had only served to send him to the boiling point. While Jack and the boys walked off, thinking all was settled, Mr. Railroader took his peeve to the town constable. When Jack noticed where the man was headed, he recommended that Allison ride out of town for the night while he and the youngster settled into Heaven. That was the night we first met our future employer, Mr. Roosevelt.

Just before closing he came in asking for a room. Though he was trying to look western, decked out in brand new a set of hunting buckskins, there was just no getting around the fact that he was a dude. Mother was hesitant to tell him that the only place we had available was Heaven. She could sense that it was not quite befitting a man of his station. But Theodore Roosevelt was as game a fellow as ever walked the west—he said Heaven would be just fine.

We were about to retire when the constable came around looking for cowboys. We sent him up to Heaven, where he barged in, ordering the whole roomful of men to get dressed for a trip to the jailhouse. Mr. Roosevelt obeyed without a word, as did Jack and his wrangler.

No sooner did Mr. Roosevelt get himself rigged up in the buckskins than the constable gave him a dubious once-over look and a dismissal. "You can get undressed and go back to bed," he said. "It's obvious *you* ain't no cowboy."

The next morning Mother took her usual breakfast basket to the jailhouse and, in her sweet Southern way, learned the whole story from the constable. Upon returning, she gave me fifty dollars from her safe-box and told me to go bail Jack out. I was so shocked by the gesture, I stared at her dumbly. "Are you feeling poorly, Mother?" I had decided illness or insanity were the only things that could pry such hard-earned cash from her grip.

"I'm fine," she told me, then smiled at me, comprehending my dumb look. "He didn't do it, honey. They've charged him with accosting a railroad worker early yesterday morning, and we both saw him bring in that herd late yesterday afternoon. I don't want him wasting away in that dirty old jailhouse."

"But, Mother, he's a cowboy. You'll never see this money returned."

"Oh, he's no cowboy, darlin'. I know Jack Stewart. He's one of my regulars. And a finer young man I've never met."

I was puzzled, but curious—which is exactly what my mother intended.

"He's educated, too," she added in a tone that was clearly meant to tantalize. "Has a law degree. He intends to defend himself and the youngster at the hearing tomorrow. I feel it only fair that the two of us should stand as witnesses on their behalf, don't you?"

Mr. Roosevelt also attended the hearing, his curiosity having been sufficiently primed by my mother as well. She was no fool. She knew it would only help Jack's case to have the justice of the peace see a man of obvious wealth sitting in his corner. And I suspect she knew I would be in love before Jack had finished presenting his case. He was really something. Even the Justice was notably impressed. A master of diplomacy, his presentation included not only an objective rendering of the muddy cigar incident—and an apology for the dance lesson—but a sympathetic understanding of the rail-worker's case of mistaken identity as well.

"It's a well-known fact, Your Honor, that cowboys all look alike to railroaders. I don't take offense at that. It would be hard for anyone to recognize differences between men when they're going thirty miles an hour. And I expect the fellas who accosted Mr. Bateson that morning before our arrival in town didn't treat him too well. And you can be assured, sir, if I knew who they were, I'd be standing here testifying for him.

"Mr. Bateson has every right to be upset by what they did and to pursue a legal recourse. However, he does *not* have the right to release his anger on an innocent boy. I will grant you that my partner may have been a bit over-zealous in coming to the boy's defense. But the boy was clearly in need of a defense.

"Here is my offer to the court, Your Honor: I will not counter-charge on the boy's behalf if Mr. Bateson withdraws his complaint and makes a simple apology to my employee, just as I am now making a simple apology to him on behalf of my partner. It should be noted, sir, that Mr. Bateson was on duty at the time of the incident, and his behavior reflects quite negatively on his employer. I doubt the District Railway Agent, Mr. Moody—who is seated over there—would take kindly to having a charge filed against the railroad because of the plaintiff's behavior."

One look from Mr. Moody in the direction of his errant employee was all it took for Mr. Bateson to issue an apology and withdraw his charges.

The Justice and I weren't the only people impressed by Jack's presentation. Mr. Roosevelt and Mr. Moody were as well, and Jack struck up an amiable friendship with both of them. Jack had been courting me for a matter of months when Mr. Moody offered him a position managing the Mandan stockyards in Dakota, which he said he would accept if I married him. We had been there a year when Mr. Roosevelt bettered the railroad's offer. That's how Jack became foreman of the Elkhorn Ranch.

The first years of our marriage there seem like paradise now, even though we both worked hard. Strenuous physical labor was simply a part of life in those days. It was the infamous winter of 1886-7 that brought the honeymoon to an end and brought us back west from Dakota. Along with nearly every rancher on the northern plains, Mr. Roosevelt suffered bad losses in the killer winter and was forced to cut back. Not one to set a good man adrift, he offered Jack a job as a clerk in his law office if we would move east. Jack respectfully declined.

In addition to the money we had saved, Jack had recently received an inheritance from the sale of his mother's headright near Austin. As a member of Stephen Austin's second colony, she had been the recipient of a land grant from the Republic of Texas, and at her death ownership was passed to her three children—Jack, Allison, and their little sister Leigh. When the community of Elgin, seeking to expand its municipality, offered them a good price for the land, they accepted. What we got wasn't much money by today's standards, but it was a tidy sum back then—enough to set us up with a small cattle business.

The cowboys who greeted us on our arrival at the homestead

had all kept up with Jack's life through Allison. Many of them had held high positions with the big cattle outfits—range bosses, wagon bosses—until the hard winter put them out of work. Being motivated men, skilled at running big ranches, they had decided to turn unemployment into an opportunity and had gone into business for themselves. Some were independent, and the others had formed a partnership, though as friends they all worked the stock together.

With so many bankruptcies in the wake of the killer winter, any cattle left to the failed syndications could be bought for a handful of cents on the dollar. Most of the group of friends had been making a good enough wage—and saving more than they drank up—and were able to buy a few head here and there. Jack had been sending Allison money to buy cattle for us so that our venture would be underway upon our arrival. We had seen ten steers wearing our JS Quarter Circle brand as we drove in and could only assume that Allison had spent our money wisely. That first evening at our new home, Jack had gotten a hint that the situation wasn't quite what it appeared, and the revelation of what our money had in truth been spent on sparked my lifelong feud with Allison.

Jack's brother was a hard-bitten character in the truest sense of the word. Life had not been kind to Allison. There had been a teenage sweetheart in Texas who died of consumption—which sent him into alternating bouts of depression and rebellion—and a shady incident thereafter, which had sent him north to escape a murder warrant. Because of his scrapes with the law, he went by only his middle name, Allison. Most people assumed it to be his last name. Cow country wasn't a place where names were questioned anyway, and at least using Allison showed more class than hiding behind something as vague as Tex or Wishbone, like some men did.

He told me early on that he did not want to besmirch his well-respected brother's reputation in our newly-chosen homeland, so I was never to recognize him as family in public. I gladly complied, though I doubt I would have claimed him even if he had insisted. No one could have deemed him and Jack to be family by looks anyway, which helped. But their differences certainly didn't stop at physical appearance.

Martin Allison Stewart had none of his brother's admirable qualities. Jack was bright, reliable, educated, a man who could speak intelligently on any number of subjects and who felt at ease in diverse groups of people. Allison, in contrast, was reclusive, prone to occluded silences, and genuinely lacking in ambition.

I do not mean to insinuate that he was lazy. He was hardly that. In many ways he was an enigma to me. There wasn't a more proficient or fearless hand on the range. As Jack said, Allison could "rope anything on anything." He had an extraordinary way with horses, as if they understood each other by some innate fusion of the soul.

The Burro Flat incident Whit Fielder had related that first night is a classic example not only of Allison's special skill with horses, but of his reckless brand of humor. Most cowboys were given to pranks in those days, and the more dangerous the better. It was a rite of passage with them. But virtually none would have risked being jerked down by roping a five-year-old maverick on an untrained horse, and certainly not for the sake of amusement. Allison was an oddity. He had no fear of God, man, or beast—or death, for that matter. His idea of a good time was chasing a family of grizzly bears into cow camp for breakfast.

His propensity for such stunts and his unequaled gift with horses won him the affection of his peers, and rightly so. While I concur with their admiration of his skill, there wasn't much else about Allison I could find worthy of anything but disdain. He had no respect for himself or his money, which never had a chance to burn a hole in his pocket—it raced him to town and spent itself wantonly on the rankest whiskey and cheapest women available, not to mention tobacco.

I hadn't one ounce of tolerance for such behavior. I'll forego a lecture on prostitution and simply state that whiskey and tobacco were the ruination of many a good man on the frontier—and cowboys were particularly vulnerable to such depravities.

But our feud didn't come about because Allison's behavior was out of the ordinary. If he wanted to race his money into town and defile himself like lesser men, so be it. It was when he elected to race *our* money into town that I took it personally. He had no right to do that. We had sent him the money to buy cattle.

Perhaps at this juncture I should explain the old range practice known as mavericking. It's a touchy subject. Depending on who you were, you might have called it by other names, such as rustling or stealing. To cowboys it was an art, and those who excelled at it were revered by their peers.

In the early days of the cow business, a top hand that was adept at bringing unmarked cattle into his boss's herd was known as a rustler. There was no negative connotation to the term then; it was simply an accepted business practice. It was impossible to decipher ownership of any full-grown head of stock that wandered the range unmarked—if it remained unbranded past weaning, it became a maverick. And there were always mavericks on the open range, because it was impossible to gather all the cattle at round-up; some were always missed. Men who came across these strays and could accomplish the task of roping and branding them for their employer were awarded a bonus of five dollars a head by the boss. The activity was known as "rustling mavericks." There was an unwritten ethic to the practice, though, which distinguishes it from what is referred to now as rustling or what could reasonably be considered stealing. The mavericker took only full-grown stuff, and the older and bigger the better. It was another rite of passage—a challenge of high skill.

Folks today often find this difficult to comprehend, because the open range cattle business is gone—the day when one top hand with two good range horses could gather and brand a dozen head of full-grown range stock single-handedly. Full mavericks were wild animals, adept at using their long, sharp horns against predators; and accomplishing the task of roping and branding them was highly dangerous work. In my own opinion, anyone skilled enough to do it should not only have rightful ownership but be given a medal in the bargain. But a woman's opinion on such matters wasn't worth much back then. In fact, the only people whose opinion did matter in the maverick issue were the associated cattlemen.

Even before the hard winter wreaked havoc on the beef industry, the associated stockgrowers were up in arms over the maverick issue, primarily because they felt as majority owners all mavericks were theirs—and they saw financial troubles ahead due to overgrazing. So many herds had been dumped onto the range by 1884 that the livestock were showing poor market weight. In an effort to meet the expectations –and Dividends—of the corporate shareholders in faraway places, many cattlemen were shipping immature stock along with the low-weight marketable stuff to conceal their financial problems and perhaps reduce the overall amount of stock on the range before disaster befell them. Of course, even under the best of circumstances, they were robbing their future profits by shipping the immature stuff—and they had no idea mother nature was going to deal them a death blow with the winter of 1886-7. At the time, they were merely scrambling to meet the bottom line.

Most of these associated cattlemen were absentee owners— British Islanders and moneyed Easterners; big businessmen accustomed to wielding wealth and political power. By nature, they had little concern for the mechanics of ranching; they measured their worth not by range skills but by numbers on a balance sheet. As long as their cowhands improved those numbers by rustling mavericks for them—and increasing their marketable stock—they were content. I suppose it was the enormous size of their herds and that imperious attitude inherent in owning wealth that led them to conclude that every maverick on the range was their exclusive property. They even had the smooth audacity to write it into law. Of course, given that the territorial legislature was comprised primarily of associated cattlemen, this was not difficult to achieve. As social men of wealth, they had little respect for the rough, lonesome ways of the cowhand. The feeling was more than mutual. These two groups moved in different worlds, a universe apart, and each tended to view the other with lively disdain.

But the maverick laws were not merely intended to settle the issue of stock ownership; they were boldly intended to elicit control of the public rangelands and put a halt to any notion of independent ranching. With an impending financial crisis on the horizon due to overgrazing, I'm sure the cattlemen felt they had no choice but to institute this control. But there was an air of panic in their writing of the laws which, in the long run, rendered them useless and fostered a rebellion. In addition to claiming every maverick in the territory for the Stockgrowers Association, the Maverick Bill forbade any employee of an associated stock outfit from owning cattle, or even the brand with which to mark them. Of course this was unconstitutional. And there was the intriguing side-issue of a private organization exacting its oppressive powers through a governmental body. In its mildest form, this type of activity is referred to these days as "catering to special interests." But to those of us who lived under its rule—and would eventually come to feel its noose on our necks—it looked a lot more like fascism, with the entire body of the Association serving as its dictator. And they got away with it for a number of years—at least they tried. The Maverick Bill was virtually impossible to enforce. The most the associated outfits could do was blackball any cowboy who owned a brand and cattle.

The situation was the equivalent of an engraved invitation to Allison. The quickest way to get that man to do anything was to tell him it was impossible. He had his brand and was blackballed before the ink was dry on the Maverick Laws. Like most Texas-bred cowboys of that era, he had been raised a Southern Democrat and had a healthy streak of Rebel in him. The custom of mavericking took on an even shinier meaning than ever when the Stockgrowers outlawed independents from practicing it.

It is an American tradition to answer tyranny with rebellion.

Allison wasn't the only cowboy drawn into business for himself simply because the Territory said he couldn't—nor was he shy about where he plied his trade. He was just as likely to gather mavericks in the presence of an Association rep as he was in the presence of his peers. It was vintage Allison, a classic response—his singular R.S.V.P to the imperious Brits and Easterners who had fabricated the laws. It said, "Come on out to the range and arrest me—if you're men enough."

If Allison wanted to acquire his cattle by mavericking, that was his prerogative as far as I was concerned. But when he decided to acquire *our* cattle that way and spend our money on self-degradation, I found it unforgivable. Along with every other independent rancher, I despised the Maverick Laws. I could readily see the unconstitutionality. But the law is the law, and I didn't believe Allison had the right to break it on our behalf. It was enough of a shock to have moved to a place that was broiling with this maverick controversy, but the fact that he had so unthinkingly cast that controversy's shadow on us by mavericking *our* cattle was, to me, unconscionable.

I had no power to change it, of course. All I could do was express my anger to Jack in the privacy of our bedchamber—a woman's only court of appeal in those days.

"I don't like the situation, either," he told me, though I know the lawyer in him admired Allison's audacity of flying in the face of tyranny.

"Mavericking his own stock is one thing, Jack. Acquiring ours that way is entirely another."

"At least he was forthright about telling us," Jack said. "Had he been a lesser man he would have concealed it."

"Had he been more of a man, he wouldn't have done it."

"Don't think too badly of him, Josie. He has an enormous amount of courage to stand up to the Association the way he's doing."

"I'm not sure an enormous lack of fear can necessarily be deemed courage, Jack. It was *wrong* of him to jeopardize our family and throw away our money on his depravities."

"I can't argue there. I'll speak to him. I intended to anyway."

"I hope you convey the extent of my anger."

He grinned. "Maybe I should just sic you on him."

"Don't think I wouldn't do it."

"Oh, I *know* you would. Your candor, darlin', is one of the things I most admire about you. But it's my responsibility. I sent him the money. It's up to me to chew him out him for spending it the way he did."

He spoke to Allison and conveyed my fury in his stern but diplomatic way. By the result of their conversation, I realized I held an element of power over Allison that was more of a frustration than his open hostility would have been. I wanted debate—contentious argument! I wanted him to attempt to defend his indefensible position. What I got was the opposite of what I expected from a fearless man, but I should have seen it coming.

Allison's admiration for Jack was enormous. I knew this from the beginning. But I never imagined that Allison could hold me in a similar regard simply for being Jack's educated wife, nor that my criticisms would elicit a reaction of meekness in a man I knew to be devoid of it. But it did. He tiptoed around my skirts forever thereafter, deferring to me so politely you would have thought I was Queen Victoria. He even bathed more often.

None of this, however, changed my opinion of him. Our private war had already begun, and I didn't view a newly-washed set of clothes and a show of humility as much of a peace offering.

CHAPTER TWO
DESCENDING INTO WAR
(Excerpt form the journal of Josie Watson Stewart)

*J*uly 20, 1889 - *Our third child was born today. A girl, finally. We named her Alexanne, after my mother who so recently passed away. It pains me unbearably that I was stuck on this remote homestead, advanced in gestation and unable to go to Mother's sickbed and see her through those last days. I have been crying for weeks, a wretched swollen heap of flesh, a bottomless well of tears, prisoner of my gender.*

July 30, 1889 - A full ten days since my last entry. Fully out of character for me, but I have seen myself slipping since long before Alexanne's arrival. This gestation was so hard, so much more difficult than Mart or Henry. I know not nor do I care whether my tears are derived from physical agony or grief. I own both in equal measure. I have lost my mother and am caught in a historic case of the baby blues, all of which has thrown me into a dark depression. My world is depressing enough. I live in a place that grows more dangerous every day, the range conflict no longer a heated war of words and posturing. News came today that a couple in a neighboring county were hanged by vigilante cattlemen for daring to own stock and file homestead claims on the open range. What have we come to that people cannot exercise their rights under the Constitution and carry on their daily lives without terror and death? Even in my numb stupor it's frightening.

Those were dark days for me. I was twenty-seven years old, physically exhausted, had a homestead and three babies to care for, and on the horizon sat innumerable worries clouding our lives like an impending thunderstorm. Oh, I was low! It's odd I can remember that day so clearly, for I was no more than a sleep-walking wraith that summer, worn to a shred from mourning my mother and bearing three children in yearly succession.

But the memory of that hot July evening is crystal clear, like a dream so strong it imprints itself as a slow-moving picture on the brain, forever illuminated, strangely off color. Perhaps it is exhaustion itself which clears away all but the meat of existence and allows for that indelible imprint of events. Even my memory of it is more the perception of an observer than a participant:

I see Jack singing a lullaby to us as I sit rocking Alexanne on the porch in the dusk, the boys already sleeping. Jack has a nice voice and often sings to us at evening time, especially now. He thinks it will help bring me back from my state of exhausted narcosis. He's a good man. I love him dearly, and I wish I could meet him halfway right now. But I'm too spent to respond.

I see Will Standifer riding up as we sit there, slowing as he approaches, quietly alighting in deference to mother and child. He speaks softly, removing his hat with kind words of greeting. His hand comes forth, offering a present for Alexanne—a painted gourd rattle. Will, Jack's best boyhood pal from Texas, is much like Jack—intelligent and perceptive. He is our closest friend. He can see me slipping away, too, and wants to do something to bring the light back into my eyes. But they're men, and have no idea what is happening to me. (They should, Lord knows—they would be the first to recognize a mare or heifer that's over-bred and needs rest.)

They feel awkward in my presence; I seem so uncharacteristically aloof to them. I don't have the energy to even muster kindness, though I manage a wan smile. Alexanne stirs and whimpers softly in my arms. Will leans over and gently shakes the rattle. Alexanne stares at the sound and hushes.

"She's a fine lookin' child, Josie," he says, handing me the toy. He steps back nodding, shy, not knowing what else to say. Like most cowboys, babies intimidate him.

Hesitating, he reaches inside his shirt and produces a newspaper, handing it to Jack. "You'd better see this," he says, pointing to an article on the front page.

Jack reads the headline "'Couple Hanged Above Horse Creek,

Prominent Stockgrowers Suspected in the Atrocity.'" He glances at Will, a look full of sudden alertness. "Dear God," he says before reading the article aloud.

It says the woman was a prostitute and cow thief, the man her paramour and accomplice. Witnesses to the double lynching have accused six local cattlemen of the crime. Warrants have been issued for their arrest.

Will glances at me, hesitates. "She wasn't what they said she was. She'd bought a handful of sore-footed stock off some immigrants passing by on the Oregon Trail. They were the only cattle she owned. It's true she and the man weren't married, but they had their reason. A married couple can only file one homestead claim, you see. Single, they could each file adjoining claims and have three hundred twenty acres when they proved-up. Problem was, their claims set smack in the middle of the favorite hay meadow of one of these 'Prominent Stockgrowers'. He tried contesting their claims, but the court awarded in favor of the couple."

The men are quiet, looking at each other, a world of shared sentiments passing unspoken between them. They step away from the porch, talking. I know they're discussing the lynching and have moved away so I won't be upset. But I'm beyond that. Emotion is gone. I have no energy left for it.

Jack is rubbing his face, deep in thought as Will speaks. Now Jack is talking. I can hear him even at this distance as if the birds and the night air have stilled solely for my benefit.

"So they created this story about her being a whore and a thief?"

Will nods dolefully "She was just a farm girl, and from what I hear she wasn't afraid of them, neither."

"What about him? What was his crime?"

"He was educated. Probably got on their wrong side when he started writing letters to the Denver newspapers trying to bring some attention to what's happening out here."

Jack breathes in deeply, sighs it out. "The cattlemen couldn't scare them away so they painted a tawdry picture and accused 'em of thievery to make the lynching appear justified. Great God, Will, what has this world come to?"

"They hung a woman, Jack. <u>A woman!</u>"

They stare at one another, their silent exchange more compelling than a blood oath.

I feel sick.

I watch as this automated likeness of myself gets up slowly, uncertainly, and sleepwalks to the bed. Lying there, I seem to float above the cabin, above the valley, looking down. A picture comes to me from this soaring height, a view of the bodies, swaying from the tree limb, swollen in the July heat, grotesque. A sob presses outward against my chest, but only comes forth as an aching sigh and a pair of tears. They are unfamiliar, these bodies, but the woman is wearing my face, the man Jack's.

A thought occurs in my numb mind that I might be better off to die then and there. Mustering the energy to live seems like a futile effort. Instead, I reach for my journal and make an entry.

It was incomprehensible to me that two people could be whisked away and disposed of so horribly. But the fact that one of them was a woman set an ominous precedent. It shook me to the core.

The crimes were appalling enough, but the aftermath proved even more terrifying. Four men had witnessed the abduction and tried to stop the lynching. One died of a sudden unknown ailment and the others mysteriously disappeared. In the end the charges against the cattlemen were dismissed for lack of evidence, and the leader of the group—the man who had coveted the dead couple's hay meadow—eventually took possession of it.

How could he live with himself, I wondered?

I tried to picture these men, the perpetrators. I knew they were much like our former employer, and I wondered what *he* thought of this atrocious series of events. News of the double hanging had been the talk of the nation—Will brought by more clippings, one from a Chicago paper, and one from San Francisco his brother had sent to him from California. The tone of the articles smacked nauseatingly of applause.

"Know what scares me?" Will said. "People in those cities'll have no choice but to believe what's in these papers—they'll think the man was a criminal and that poor woman was sellin' favors to every cowboy in a hundred miles in exchange for stolen livestock."

Jack stood from the table pensively. "If you think that scares you, Will, step back and look at a broader context. Think of the inference. If the cattlemen can get public opinion behind them with these falsities, what does that tell you they have in mind for the cowboys who supposedly stole the stock with which to curry her alleged favors?"

The two men locked gazes across the table.

"What this tells me," Jack said, pointing to the papers, "is that the cattlemen have made an official declaration of war on every independent rancher in this Territory."

Will stared at him, then looked my way.

"Do you really believe that?" I asked Jack.

"Yes. Much as I hate to say it, I do. I've been following this thing ever since the lynching. I've talked to people who knew the couple—the man had gone to Cornell. I read the articles he sent to the Denver papers. He was very outspoken in his disdain of the cattlemen and their tyranny. They wanted to shut him up, and this is how they chose to do it. But they had to get public opinion behind them to derive at least a cultural justification of what they've done. When I look at these articles decrying him as a vicious criminal, something very odd strikes me."

"Odd?—it's a pack of lies!" said Will. "That's more than just odd."

"Of course it's lies, and that's part of it—but look deeper. In every one of these articles his name has been misspelled in the exact same way. That tells me the information that went to all the national papers came from one source. This"—Jack gestured to the clippings on the table—"is a press release."

"You're speakin' college talk, Jack," said Will. "Speak regular American."

"When an organization has a story for publication and they want it told their own way, they prepare the story themselves and give it to the press. Granted, it's usually something innocuous in nature, not a double homicide. But look at it. This is not journalism. Where—in all of these national papers—is the real story? Where does it tell of the court contest that the dead couple won against their killer? Where does it say that the dead man had publicly given voice to the tyranny we're living under? Where does it say that the witnesses to the lynching have mysteriously died or disappeared? It's not there. What's there is fiction."

"I don't know why that should surprise you," said Will. "They've been manufacturing laws to suit their interests—why not manufacture stories, too?"

"But this is more ominous even than their laws, Will. Laws we can fight. Subverted credibility is extremely hard to overcome. Step back for a minute and really look at this. You said yourself, the people in the cities will have no choice but to believe these stories. Don't you see what the cattlemen are doing? They're setting a stage. They're telling the world—under the guise of newspaper reporting—that cowboys are low-life thieves and the settlers in Wyoming are criminals and prostitutes. "

I looked soberly at Jack. "Do you think this means they've got more of this kind of thing already planned?"

"I don't know if they've got it planned yet or not. But it means they are determined to have things their way, and nothing will stop them—not you, not me, not the laws that forbid them from coveting another person's property and even killing that person to get it."

It was like living in a nightmare. Again I tried to imagine how Mr. Roosevelt would view this awful affair, and I even thought of writing to him. But we had lost touch, drifted apart, and whether I wanted to admit it or not, I knew events had thrown us on opposite sides of an issue so controversial it had become deadly. The whole situation bred a haunting suspicion that crept into every area of our lives, to the extent that a once-trusted friend fell under the pall of doubt merely because of his business and his wealth. The terror was that pervasive. Try as I might, though, I could never in my wildest imagination put his face on one of the hangmen.

I was too exhausted to remember how we muddled on, but we did somehow. Sensing that my return to normalcy depended somewhat on him, Jack assumed responsibility for Mart, taking him along on his chores around the place and even riding him out to the range sometimes. Mart always did seem older than his age, and would forever thereafter cut the figure more of an adult than a child.

Things seemed to quiet down after the double lynching, although no one was fool enough to believe the range troubles were over. There was just a moratorium on overt acts for awhile, I guess. But there was a tension in the air that was almost palpable.

Even though guns were expensive, Jack bought another one— over my strenuous objections. He had tried and tried to get me to keep a revolver, but I refused. He wore his all the time by then, as did anyone who worked the range. But I wouldn't have one in the house. Good grief, I had three small children toddling about—what if one of them should find it? There are few things on this earth I despise more than a handgun, and I wasn't about to let the situation, dire though it was, intimidate me into packing one.

He bought me a Winchester carbine instead—for hunting, he said, although I hadn't hunted since Dakota. It was shorter than the old Springfield, easier to handle, quicker to load and fire. I wasn't fooled by his 'hunting' explanation, of course. I knew he had bought me the rifle to shoot cattlemen with. But I was certain in my stubborn youthful conceit that if any cattlemen showed up with a noose and an arsenal I could disarm them with my wit and intelligence alone. I had regained most of my strength by then and was back on my high horse.

Along with the tense air of suspicion which followed in the wake of the lynching incident, there was also a swell of alliance among the homesteaders. It was more or less a spontaneous phenomenon, akin to the solidarity which springs up in response to most forms of oppression. Just as there was a grapevine among the black slaves in the South, we developed our own covert form of communication. For instance, if the right half of a stable door was open it meant there were cattlemen or their sympathizers in the vicinity and to tread softly and keep your mouth shut; if the left half was open it meant the homestead was safe to approach.

The similarity between our situation and other forms of oppression was not lost on us. As soon as the cattlemen injected every possible negative connotation into the term 'rustler' and referred to the independent ranchers wholesale as such, our men began referring to the cattlemen as 'white caps'—an allusion to the Ku Klux Klan.

Trustworthiness became increasingly difficult to discern. Cowboys were by nature avidly loyal to their employers and openly affable with their peers. Many deep friendships had been formed among the men who worked the range together, before the hard winter had blown in with its troubles. The burgeoning war placed a divisive strain on the working hands' natural tendencies, for if a man remained loyal to his employer it meant forsaking the trust of his blackballed pals.

Will Standifer was one of the only men on the range who managed to maintain both a working relationship with the big outfits and implicit trust with his own group. His was a unique situation, though. Will was more than a top hand; he was capable of running a big outfit, and his trenchant honesty had made him a favored employee among the cattlemen. He was a gifted range boss, and some of the cattlemen broke their own rules by hiring him periodically after the hard winter, even though he was already running his own herd. Had he been a man of less integrity, he would never have garnered such trust.

Most cowhands had no economic choice but to ride for the brand of an employer, and yet their natural sympathies tended to run with the independent ranchers. The best of them were men who, while working loyally in silence, were able to disclose their affiliation by some small deed here or there. And, conversely, there were men whose loyalty rested firmly with an employer. Most of such fellows were not resented by the independents, their stance was thoroughly understood. They were, for the greater part, men who attempted to steer clear of the range controversy and simply do their jobs.

There were among them, though, men who abused their friendship with the independents by becoming spies for their employers. Every society has such characters—people who deem it their purpose in life to ingratiate themselves to whoever is in power. I believe the modern colloquial term for this type of individual is a 'brown nose'. While I'm not given to colloquialisms, it is such an apt term I feel compelled to employ it with regard to these spies. I opine that the bulk of their gray matter and the sum of their moral tissue were comprised of the very substance that made their noses brown.

I wasn't alone in feeling so strongly. Jack despised them, as did all our circle of friends—with the exception of Will Standifer. It was the only issue on which Jack and Will vehemently disagreed. Will tended to throw these spies in the same pot with all the other cowboys who were simply exhibiting loyalty to a brand. Even when one such fellow, Mike Finn, betrayed him in a manner that was fully intended to be lethal, Will shrugged and tolerated. He was a truly amazing man. In a less earthy profession, he would have come off as seeming uncannily Christ-like—this 'turn the other cheek' attitude was wholly genuine. Jack could not understand that. To him the spies, and Finn in particular, were lower than scum.

And then there were the stock detectives.

They were worse than scum's underside. They spied for a living—and a mighty lucrative one at that. I make no attempt to disguise my hatred for these individuals. I suppose there must have been good-hearted, good-natured stock detectives somewhere. But I never knew of them. So I must proceed from the only perspective I know: my own experience. And I will state unequivocally that I am not nor can I be unbiased where stock detectives are concerned.

Ed Weston.

As difficult as it is for me to talk about this man, I will attempt to corral my rancor enough to portray an accurate picture of him, because he is a central character in this drama.

Weston owned many of the same personality traits as another nefarious character whose name was anathema to settlers, Tom Horn. They were both men of gregarious charm; cunning and intelligent, both had nerves of steel, both operated with self-chosen precision on either side of the law, both were paid stock detectives, and they owned not one single iota of morality between the two of them. Not only did they spy for a living, they murdered for a living.

To the settler population, they were known as back-shooters—the most disparaging term in the Westerner's vocabulary. It has always been my contention that someone should have done the world a favor by introducing them to one another, in a locked room, where they could do their nefarious work on each other. It would have saved us all a universe of pain.

Weston had come here virtually out of nowhere in the early days of the cattle boom and, as sheriff, endeared himself to the sparse population of the county by being tough on outlaws. There weren't many outlaws to be tough on in those days, but the few that existed wished they had never made the acquaintance of Ed Weston. Many people considered his tactics more appropriate for a bounty hunter than a sheriff, but Weston couldn't have cared less about such opinions. What counted to him was that he was making quite an impression on the owners of power and wealth—the cattlemen. By the time we arrived in 1887, Weston had long been in the secret employ of the Association as their chief stock detective.

I'll never forget the night in late September of '89 when Jack came home from a long stretch on the range. The children were already sleeping. I fixed him some food and set it before him on the table. He stared at it blankly.

"Jack?" I said softly. "Are you alright?"

He looked at me. "I met Ed Weston today."

Foremost of the information on the settler grapevine was the identity of known spies and stock detectives, so I was already acquainted with the name. Stories of Weston abounded among the settlers—the most infuriating to me being the one about the milk cow.

When the Association round-ups came through, the settlers had to get their cattle out of the way or risk losing them. For if our cattle were gathered with the big round-ups our brands were vented, our cattle marked as mavericks and sold to the highest bidder—the money going to the Association's market seizure fund. Even though our brands were registered with the county, they were not Association brands and they considered theirs the only legal brands on the range. To claim any money from the market seizure fund, a person had to prove ownership of the cattle that were sold, and since—to them—our brands were not lawful, we could not claim ownership for what they had stolen from us. How did they get away with such tyranny? They controlled the legislature, which stipulated that Association round-ups were the only legal round-ups—and independent ranchers could not participate.

And they called *us* thieves.

I know this sounds like strange fiction, but these things really happened.

The milk cow belonged to a farmer. It was the only cow he owned and was penned by his stable—obviously a milk cow, obviously owned and not wandering the range. Weston came along and sat horseback by the pen looking the animal over. When the farmer came out of the stable to greet him and invite him to supper, Weston dropped a loop over the pen and tore it open.

"What're you doin', mister?" the farmer demanded.

Weston replied, "That creature's unbranded. You know all mavericks belong to the Association." And he took the milk cow with the round-up.

I thought of this when Jack said he had met Weston and wondered what manner of intimidation the skunk had tried on my husband. "You met him on the range? What did he do?" I asked.

"He attempted to shake my hand," Jack said, and abruptly stood up. He paced back and forth along the table.

This was more than anger at having been introduced to the chief of stock detectives. Something had happened. Finally he sat, staring at the light of the coal oil lamp.

"When I was practicing law down in Austin," he said, "we prosecuted a crime that was the worst thing I ever saw. An elderly couple had been murdered over some insurance money. And not killed quickly, either."

"Oh, Jack!"

"We had a clear case against the suspect," he went on, "a young man who had befriended the old couple. They were childless and took him under their wing—adopted him, more or less—and named him their beneficiary. I interviewed him twice after the murder. He was a cool customer. He never admitted to it, but I knew he had done it. And he *knew* I knew it."

Jack shook his head, remembering. "It's hard to describe him, Jose. There was not one trace of remorse—it was scary how completely lacking in conscience the man was. The day we got the warrant issued, he disappeared."

Suddenly I dreaded what his next words might be.

He looked at me. "That man's real name is *not* Ed Weston."

"Oh, my Lord," I gasped. I stared at Jack, trying to imagine what he had thought when Weston offered his hand. "Did he know who you were?"

Jack nodded.

"And he knew you recognized him as well?"

"There wasn't so much as a shadow of doubt."

I was scared. "What will you do, Jack?"

He stood and began pacing again. "I don't know. I went straight to Ally and cussed him out for not telling me who Weston was before this."

"Allison knew?"

"He's known all along."

It was another reason to despise my brother-in-law, as far as I was concerned. "Allison has been here for years—why in the world hasn't he said anything?"

"What could he say, Jose? He can't run to the authorities and tattle-tale about a Texas murder warrant on the chief stock detective when there's one for *him* sitting down in the Capitol right now. If he opened his head about this, Weston would turn the tables on him faster than you could blink. And Ally would be the one to end up in a noose, you could bet on it."

I was angry now. "So you're willing to let the two of them maintain this conspiracy of silence? We're talking about *murder*, Jack."

"Ally's case was self-defense," he countered. "I know he's my brother, Jose, but I speak solely as a lawyer when I say there is nothing remotely similar about the charges in their two cases."

"Really," I declared. "Well, if Allison is so innocent, why hasn't he ever made an attempt to be acquitted?"

"You don't understand the situation."

"No, I don't. I believe you'll need to enlighten me, darlin'."

Jack had never spoken of the charges against Allison. It was one of those deep, silent family things that never see the light of day. He was disinclined to speak of it even then, but I had left him little choice. He would have to explain to me why he was not on his way to the authorities that very moment with testimony as to Ed Weston's identity.

He sat down, stared at the lamp again. "Ally wasn't always wild. In fact, he was kind of shy as a kid. The two of us were always close, but it was our little sister Leigh that Ally felt was his particular responsibility as he grew older, especially with me gone off to college and Mother ill. I suppose the combination of Mother dying and Father remarrying was the turning point. He never got along with our step-mother, you see. But when the family came out so adamantly against his alliance with the Condron girl, he went over the rim. We should never have done that. He loved her. He truly did."

This was more than Jack had ever said about his family. One's kin was taboo as a conversational topic back then. But the thought of Allison in love and teetering breathlessly on the cusp of marriage was more than I could picture. I had to pursue. I was too intrigued. "Why were the family against it?"

"Oh, Donie was a nice girl—came from a fine family—but she had consumption, and we were afraid she would infect him too. Leigh was the only one who backed him. She told me later that Ally cried and cried when the family went against him. He told her he only wanted to make Donie happy for whatever time she had left. I reckon it was the last tear he intended to shed, though. He was in trouble constantly from then on. I was away at college during all of this, but I managed to put my two-cents in by letter and destroy his happiness along with the rest of the family. I find it ironic now that, while we were so afraid she would infect him with consumption, we ourselves infected him with this destructive rebellion. And I regret it."

I never expected that I could actually feel sympathy for Allison. But I did at that moment. He was clearly the family tragedy. I touched Jack's hand. "Darlin', your two-cents did not send Allison along the wayward path."

He took my hand in his. "I know. But it goes deeper than that. All our lives I was somehow the one who got every advantage. It was more than being the oldest son. Sure, I got the new clothes—Ally got the hand-me-downs. But I also got the good horses, Ally got the old plugs. I got the college education, Ally barely got through grammar school. I don't know why Father neglected him so, but he always did. I used to think it was the difference in our looks, but I could never figure out whether it was that Father resented Ally for favoring our mother or simply loved me because I resembled him. Either way, it doesn't make any sense. What would make a man show such blatant favoritism, Jose? Allison never deserved that treatment."

I shook my head, shrugged helplessly. "Maybe it wasn't deliberate," I offered. "Your mother was ill. Perhaps it wasn't so different from what we've had to do this summer while I was recovering—you taking Mart along with you while I looked after Henry and the baby."

I don't think he even heard me.

It was obvious that his compulsion to protect Allison was based on a guilt sown by an unthinking parent in childhood. But the Jack I knew and loved wouldn't let even *that* get in the way of justice. Would he? He must have seen the question in my eyes.

He fiddled with my fingers a moment, lacing them absently in his own. "I was the one who advised Allison to leave Texas rather than face the murder charge," he said.

"Was the advisement given as his brother or his attorney?"

"Both," he sighed. "I don't even know how the argument started, but some way or another Ally got cross-wise with a couple of cowboys—probably over a card game. Allison was working for a neighbor, and one day while he and the neighbor's son were out in the brush gathering stock, four fellas came looking for Allison. Tempers flared. Shots were fired, and the boy with Ally was wounded. Well, that really made Ally mad. Here, the kid was just working with him—had no connection to the argument—and these birds come along and open fire on him. So Allison fought back. Pulled his pistol and shot one of them dead, wounded a second. The others took cover and commenced firing. You know, Allison could have left that boy, but he didn't. He risked his life to get him to safety. The other men had them pinned down for several hours. During that time, the boy died."

"Well, it certainly sounds like you could build a good case of self-defense. Why would you advise Allison to leave?"

"It wasn't a simple situation, Josie. He already had some drunk and disorderly arrests, one involving a pistol. None of the other men had records. And the second man he wounded eventually died as well, so there were two killings to contend with."

"Don't you mean three—what about the boy? Certainly *they* were charged with a killing, too?"

Jack shook his head. "While one of the men had Allison pinned down, the other ran to the authorities and told them Ally and the boy had jumped *them*. Given he had no prior record, his story was believed."

"Allison was a witness," I argued, "he could have counter-charged, and should have if the truth was on his side."

"It was two to one, Jose. Their word against his."

"The truth should be stronger than that old excuse for inaction."

"It's certainly a fact that Allison was a witness," he explained patiently, "but he had a record, which included assault with a deadly weapon. The other men, in having no prior occurrences, had more credibility to present to a jury. Allison was a known troublemaker. His case was too weak to win, Jose."

"Well," I demurred, "I'm not a lawyer, so you'll pardon me if I happen to believe telling the truth is better than running away, no matter what the circumstances. I'm not criticizing you, Jack. I just disagree is all."

Wan shadows in the surrounding darkness left the lamp illuminating only his face, shadowed yet clearly in a quandary.

"I regretted having advised him to leave, but I didn't know what else to do. He didn't deserve to go to jail and he didn't have a winnable case. The whole thing—and the case with the old couple who were murdered—gave me a bad taste for practicing law. That's really why I left it, Jose—sure, I didn't like working indoors. But who would when you're faced with cases like that? I just—I didn't expect it to come back and haunt me. But it has."

Fear welled up at the thought of Weston. "Jack"—I squeezed his hand—"I understand that you want to protect Allison, and I can't pass judgment on whether that's right or wrong. You did what you thought was best. But I have a bad feeling about Weston. If he killed two old people, he could stalk and kill you too just for knowing who he is."

Jack shook his head. "He made casual reference to the charges against Allison when we spoke today. I guess that was his way of telling me he'd use the knowledge as a hole card if I thought of turning him in. But I'll be cautious, you can count on that."

I wanted to rant on—Jack had a wife and children to consider and the only safe and decent thing to do was go to the authorities. I wanted to leap to my feet and yell that I was tired of living on the edge of sanity, that this range war was ruining our lives—that our children didn't even know what curtains were, for pity sake! They thought it was *normal* to black out windows with blankets every night so no one inside could become a target. They thought it was *normal* for adults to go around loaded for bear. They thought it was *normal* to never trust a stranger and never *ever* answer any of his questions.

They thought terror was normal.

Fear is a paradoxical animal. It makes you want to rave in

hysterics and calmly deny its very existence both at the same time. It makes you want to laugh and cry all in one breath. Perhaps I should have let my head strength match my fear at that moment. Perhaps I should have stood straight up and let it all fly out of my mouth unedited.

But we didn't do such things back then. As headstrong and outspoken as I was, I wasn't ready to be branded as a crazy woman. So I did what most women did in those days. I persevered in silence.

CHAPTER THREE
RUSTLERS AND WHITE CAPS
(Excerpt from the journal of Josie Watson Stewart)

*O*ctober 1, 1889 - We have a hired hand. He's just a boy of thirteen, the son of a family newly- arrived from Kansas who have settled some ten miles away under the long red wall. They have many children, plenty of helping hands, and at least one too many mouths to feed. Jack offered to take Dudley for the fall and winter seasons. Now I will have someone with me so Jack won't have to worry when he's out tending the cattle. Dudley is a hard worker and a fast learner. In return for his labors I am teaching him to read and write. He was a little shocked to find that Mart, who is not yet four, already knows his numbers and letters. Perhaps it will be good incentive for Dudley to study hard and catch up.

October 10, 1889 - A strange incident happened today. Stranger still, Jack asked me not to write about it in my journal—as if anyone were going to see what I write! We argued over it vigorously. I'm still in a state of high vexation and tempted to write about it anyway. If we hadn't mutually agreed to a moratorium on our matrimonial intimacies because of my physical exhaustion, I would surely insist on it tonight!

I can remember that evening with a smile now, but—oh—I was fit to be tied just then. It was the first time Jack and I had what could really be defined as an argument. We had debated issues before, but never *that* vehemently.

In retrospect, Jack was correct in not wanting me to write about it. At least he was correct at that juncture in history. He always did have the ability to think within the broader context of a situation and act appropriately. Now, with so much water under the bridge and out of an interest in depicting the period accurately, I feel the time has come to exhume the incident, warts and all, if for no other reason than for posterity.

Dudley hadn't been with us more than a week or so. The men were due back from fall round-up and I had baked a dozen loaves of bread. I asked Dudley to saddle up and ride down two homesteads below us with some loaves for the Johnson boys, who were bachelors and would appreciate the gesture. It was three miles away, an hour or so round trip. He did as I asked and returned, looking as if he had seen a gaggle of ghosts.

"What is it, Dudley?" I asked. Those days any number of spooky things could have taken place in three miles.

"Your neighbor, Mrs. Stewart, the one just yonder. He come out with a rifle and told me I couldn't ride through his gate no more. Said none of us could."

"Why, that's silly! It's the only road in and out of here. We have to use it, Dudley. Mr. Burgee has no right to stop us."

"Yes'm. But I b'lieve he'll try. He seemed awful worked up about it."

The man he was referring to, John Burgee, was our closest neighbor, discounting Allison, who rarely slept on his claim.

I am uncertain exactly where the parting of the ways originated between Burgee and the friends. Some have said he was always jealous of the others, felt himself an outsider as a West Virginian, and chose to respond by lording his education over them. I couldn't dispute or defend that, but I know all the others had come from Williamson county and there's one trait common to all Texas cowboys—they subscribe wholesale to the notion that "if you ain't from Texas, you ain't a cowboy."

Here is what I do know for certain. Long before we left Dakota five of our group had all joined as partners in a single brand, the Boot Five. They were Whit Fielder, Ben Lattis, Billy Shaw, John Burgee, and Allison. They were the first five men blackballed—the Original Sinners from the Association's perspective; to their peers, the nerviest men on the range. They had filed a homestead claim next to Allison's and built a ranch. Our secluded valley had hay-meadows, good water, and direct access to the high country parks.

Burgee, by reason of his education, had elected himself account keeper of the Boot Five. As an outsider, he would have had to assert himself among that group of Texans, but he was a bullheaded man by nature anyway. Whether his drinking habit was acquired as a defense against so much Texas arrogance or he brought it with him from West Virginia, I don't know. I do know that alcohol made him more bullheaded than usual.

By the end of '88 Lattis and Shaw were concerned that Allison and Burgee were drinking up too much of the Boot Five's profits. And they didn't wholly trust Burgee with the accounts since he was in his cups a good deal of the time. With Whit Fielder's permission, they demanded dissolution of the partnership. Jack mediated the negotiations.

They had no problem with Allison, who always was first to admit to his depravities—and who also had his own homestead claim anyway. Burgee was another story. He put up a heated quarrel, spiked with a threat of lawsuit, and if it weren't for Jack's levelheaded diplomacy the situation could have turned ugly. In the end Allison got most of the partnership's horses, Lattis and Shaw got the brand and most of the cattle, and Fielder and Burgee got the ranch and a portion of the hoofed assets apiece.

Lattis and Shaw simply moved the Boot Five's headquarters one valley over and continued their partnership. Whit Fielder decided to work the range out along Salt Creek and South Fork, and we didn't see much of him for awhile. Burgee married a widow with three children, and brought them to the ranch house. He sold a little hay until he could get a few more head of cattle together, which he preferred to keep in our valley or the high parks rather than on the open range.

He never said anything about having Allison's claim directly upstream, probably because having Allison for a neighbor was like having no neighbor at all. But our homestead sat above Allison's on the valley's best hay-meadow and hindered Burgee's access to the high country parks. Evidently, that got to bothering Burgee, and the longer he thought about it, the more it irked him. But I had no inkling of his true feelings until the incident with Dudley.

I don't know why Burgee never said anything before. I have wondered over it many times because, as I say, he was a contentious man. I can only assume that, having been raised in a Southern gentlemanly tradition, he never said anything to me out of a polite deference to gender. Jack, I'm certain, had his respect—though perhaps grudging—because of owning a higher education than himself. And we were neighbors in a remote country, so I assume he felt the most appropriate demeanor was to act like good neighbors even if your thoughts ran in a different vein.

I knew he was prone to drink more than the average family man, and I guessed correctly that he had been drinking when Dudley happened by. Jack arrived shortly thereafter and I told him what had happened. He didn't even unsaddle. He told Dudley to hitch up the wagon and ride down to the Johnson place again, then turn around and come back. Dud was clearly afraid to do it, but Jack helped him hitch up and assured him that everything would be fine. To give him added assurance, he placed Martin on the wagon seat as well.

"Nobody in their right mind would hurt a child," he told Dud confidently.

I almost fainted. I wanted to scream a protest that a drunken man was not *in* his right mind and grab my son from that wagon. But Jack backed me off with a hug that curtained my fearful look from Dudley.

"Don't worry," Jack whispered in my ear.

Little Mart was stoic as a sentry, which gave Dud incentive to swallow his fear and commence the undertaking. Soon as they disappeared beyond the trees, Jack slipped some cartridges in the Winchester and mounted up.

"What on earth are you doing!" I panicked.

He leaned down and kissed me, cool as a cucumber. "Nobody's going to get hurt, Josie. I promise."

I watched him go, wishing I could feel so confident. The worst mixture in the world is alcohol and firearms. I ran to the corral and climbed up where I had a clear view of the wagon trail. I could see the gate a quarter mile below and the wagon approaching it, but Jack had disappeared somewhere in the trees.

Child though he was, Mart remembered that incident with uncommon clarity to his dying day. He was too young to be frightened like Dudley; he knew there was something important going on, but he didn't know what. When they reached the gate and Burgee stepped forward with a shotgun, Mart comprehended the ominous nature of the situation. But before he had time to get scared his father suddenly appeared, Winchester at the ready, and placed his horse between Burgee and the wagon.

"Evenin', John," Jack said cheerfully, then waved Dudley on. "You boys go ahead with your errand. I need to get Mr. Burgee's opinion on something."

Dud gladly drove on as Jack dismounted, slipped an arm through Burgee's as if they were the best of friends, and strolled toward his house.

I was baffled from my distance, but I could see my fear had apparently been misguided. So I went back to the children and the chores and waited. The boys returned at dusk, but still no Jack. I fixed supper, trying not to worry. The boys ate and I put the younger children to bed while Jack's supper got cold. And I waited. The boys fed the horses, washed up and studied before going to bed. I went then to the porch, sat in the rocker with my journal and tried to be calm.

And I waited.

I was just about to risk death and go demand to know of Mr. Burgee what he had done with my husband's body when I heard the unmistakable tones of the Civil War tune "Lorena" coming from the wagon path. It was Jack's favorite song, and he was doing it rare justice. Presently he appeared in the moonlight, rode to the porch, and swept off his hat in exaggerated courtesy.

"Lovely evenin', Mrs. Stewart. Care to dance?"

I stood to my feet, shocked and mad as a wet cat. "Jackson Alfred Stewart, you're drunk!"

"No. But I'm durn close," he said, dismounting. "Don't go too hard on me, Josie. I had to do it. It was necessary to the negotiation."

"I have been sitting here worried to distraction that our neighbor had hacked you to pieces for stew-meat, and all this time you've been getting drunk with him!"

"I think you'll forgive me, darlin', when you hear my story. Sit down and I'll tell you about the magnificent feat of diplomacy I just accomplished."

I plopped myself down in the rocker and stared at him coldly.

I must admit that the story he told was truly amazing. He had opened his conversation with Burgee by appealing to their common link as educated family men in discussing the range conflict, ignoring any notion that a dispute over ingress and egress existed between them. Specifically, Jack wanted to elicit Burgee's support in a practice he felt was imperative to initiate among the settlers and independent ranchers.

Thus appealed to, Burgee was all ears.

Jack told him he deemed it essential that everyone should present a united front to the cattlemen and indeed to the world—solidarity that went beyond the spontaneous cohesion already forming. The only way to accomplish such a feat, he contended, was for everyone to put aside their differences and work together for the common goal of justice—and he managed to convey this without inferring that any such differences existed between the Stewarts and the Burgees.

"At stake, John," Jack stressed, "is our freedom, the safety of our families, and—let's face it—our own lives. You and I are educated men. We have the intellectual tools necessary to lead this call to solidarity."

"That's true," Burgee nodded thoughtfully.

"I realize it's no small thing that I'm proposing. It'll likely draw some unwanted attention our way."

"Undoubtedly. It will."

"On the other hand, we couldn't live up to our citizenship very easily if we ignored injustice or bowed to tyranny. James Madison and the boys gave us more than a magnificent piece of paper when they designed the Constitution. They knew in order for that document to work, it would require the vigilance of every generation that came after them. We have children, John. We can't leave them less than what we were given."

"I certainly can't argue there."

"This movement needs your expertise. You've been in this country longer than most. What do you say? Will you lead it with me?"

Burgee thought for a moment. "I'm glad to know you're a thinking man, Jack. I had about given up on having an intellectual discussion with anyone in these parts. Yes, as hard as they'll probably make things for us, I'm willing to step into the fire with you. There is just one thing I'd like to ask in return."

"Ask away, neighbor."

"I'd like permission to cross your land to get my cattle to and from the high country."

"Permission granted gladly, John. We'll establish a trail along the west side of the valley that we can both use."

The subtle magnitude of what Jack had accomplished is expressed in the thoroughness of both his actions and his presentation. By having Dudley pass through the gate in the presence of both Burgee and himself, he had legally settled the issue of ingress and egress when he cordially walked Burgee toward the house. By appealing to Burgee's intellect on the range conflict, he opened an issue that only men of like mind and mutual confidence could address. I have often wondered if Burgee ever realized how deftly Jack neutralized his peeve.

Naturally, I was proud of Jack's accomplishment—except for the drinking—and wanted to champion his talents in my journal. That's when the argument started. Jack would not allow it.

"I don't want the opposition to see anything on our side but total solidarity," he said. "If they know there's a dispute among us, it's an invitation for them to ram in a wedge and tear us apart. Divide and conquer, Jose."

"What about the split-up of the Boot Five," I argued. "That's common knowledge from here to the capital and I don't notice the cattlemen making an issue of it."

"That's because we've been very careful to portray it as an amiable parting of the ways for the cattlemen's benefit. Nobody knows but the partners and us that there was an issue of drinking and gambling at the core of the split. And that's the way it must remain."

"And you think my journal is going to be some great revelation for the cattlemen? Need I remind you that it's a private record?"

"I know that, Josie, and I didn't mean to insinuate that you would ever reveal anything to them. But they have to view us as united in every way, or we'll be a lost cause before we even start. And the solidarity has to appear spontaneous. That's imperative. I can't allow you to document its planning."

"You say that as if I were going to publish my diary in the *Livestock Journal*," I huffed, referring to the Association's publication. "For heaven's sake, Jack, I don't even let *you* read it! I'm not writing it for your benefit or even my own! I'm doing it for our grandchildren—who won't even appear for another quarter century and who probably won't give a hoot about any of these damned range troubles anyhow!"

Well, that did it. I had never cursed at him before, and that one word held him speechless for at least a minute.

"I know this seems like a feeble argument to you, Josie," he finally entreated, "but I beg of you, please don't write it down. We're involved in something of enormous significance here, and we need to act in a certain fashion and never even let our *grand*children know we planned it that way. It's important. Please understand that."

Although I understood some of his reasoning from the beginning, I felt his descent into a night of alcohol gave me a perfect right to argue as loudly and as long as I pleased. And I pleased to argue vigorously just then. I had to release all that pent-up anxiety somehow. The leap from thinking Burgee had pulled a Lizzie Borden on Jack to seeing him come home drunk was a bit more than my frayed nerves could take.

For five glorious minutes I threw caution to the wind, risked the brand of craziness, and let all those unmentionable things come sailing out of me: the drinking, the frazzling effect of the range conflict, the fear inherent in knowing Weston's identity, the exhaustion of raising three babies simultaneously.

But when it came to my attention that my diatribe was being quietly absorbed by Mart, his face a small oval of frightened wonderment in the darkness, I became an instant mother again. Smiling sweetly, I tucked Martin back in, closed my mouth and acquiesced stonily to Jack's wishes.

If I hadn't felt that he was trying to control a part of me he had no right to touch—my inner thoughts, my *journal*—I would have acquiesced amiably. I probably shouldn't even have mentioned it to him. But, silly me, I thought in view of his inebriation I was tossing him an olive branch by attempting to champion his diplomacy to posterity.

In my anger, it never occurred that the only way the cattlemen could have ever known of the journal's existence was by raiding our home. Implicit in that thought would have been Jack's fear that such a thing was distinctly possible. He was more deeply concerned for our future than I knew just then.

And he was right in every argument he employed that night. The cattlemen would have used any disagreement among us settlers to highlight our faults, and they had prodigious ways of doing such things. They had managed to besmirch the reputations of that couple they lynched, planting abominable articles in newspapers from one end of the nation to the other. Even at this late date, it has been deemed by some as chancy to reveal what I have just revealed, because there has always been a feeling among the settlers and their descendents that retribution from the cattlemen's press machine could somehow escape the passage of the time and death.

Whether that proves to be true or not, I am compelled to go forward out of my own sense of truth. The fact that solidarity was a conscious choice was, to me, more admirable than any natural cohesion could ever have been. That people would actually set aside their differences in the name of a higher cause seems to me infinitely more praiseworthy than spontaneity.

And I feel it is time people understand that, contrary to the cattlemen's formidable propaganda, we were *not* a ragtag gaggle of ignorant clodhoppers, whores and rebel thieves. To measure the success of their press machine, one need only look at how prevalent—even today—their rendering of this image is in Western fiction: cowboys are all too often depicted as low-life thieves, and it's a rare woman who isn't a prostitute.

Their tyranny was not only grounded in 'ruling class' prejudice—the haves against the have-nots—or the arrogance of big business. There was a strong political axiom in their malevolence as well. Most of the cattlemen were Yankee Republicans while many of the settlers were Southern war refugees, and the vast majority of the independent cowboys were Texas Democrats.

We may have been by and large ordinary people, but we did not lie quietly in the face of tyranny. And most of us tried to meet the challenges with integrity. There was a greater degree of ethics and diplomacy exhibited in that one conversation between Burgee and Jack than the cattlemen's association would demonstrate in all the nineteenth century.

I certainly don't mean to infer that our side had a monopoly on morality. I still say today the same thing about the range war that I said when it finally ended: there was right on both sides and there was wrong on both sides. To my knowledge, there were no angels among the ranks of either the independent ranchers or the cattlemen. As Whit Fielder put it in 1920, "The only place where we really had the best of it was we never lynched a soul nor shot anyone in the back. And nobody in our group went to killin' beef till the white caps went to killin' men."

For years before the first casualty fell in the range war, we had been accused wholesale of enormous depredations on the cattle herds, not just mavericking but beefing as well, the killing of stock for meat. It was generally assumed by the cattlemen that settlers were natural-born beefers and not to be trusted as anything else. This was a dual prejudice, both political and social, derived of the supposition that we Southerners would sneak any economic retaliation for the loss of the Civil War, and that as people of modest means, we coveted their wealth and would steal whatever of it we could. One need not be a present day psychologist to perceive the elements of guilty fear and projection inherent in their prejudice.

I will not deny that there were cattle thieves on the range, men who would take stock without qualm. That type of individual existed wherever there was open range. For the most part they were men of the drifting sort who had no ties, no scruples, and who were adept at living on the edge of lawlessness. I can think of three in our area who were known to have robbed a train.

Unfortunately, as cowhands they were identified with our side, and the cattlemen pointed to them as prime examples of thievery—rightly so. Unfortunate as well is the fact that many of these individuals were former co-workers of the men on our side, and they abused that relationship by taking full advantage of the range situation to further their own nefarious aims. They assumed rudeness as a birthright, killed beef and sold it to whoever would pay for it, and in general muddied the waters of our cause irreparably. The cattlemen had a perfect right to yell "Thief!" at such men. But when they did, their epithets landed on us—their inference of "guilt by association" was, of course, fully intentional. They used those men's actions to fuel their fires of aggression.

I still resent those men. They complicated an already complex issue.

But I suppose every conflict has such border lopers—the ones who loot in a riot, those men of no conscience and considerable devilment. We were their victims as much as the cattlemen's. Their actions lent a sense of validation to the aggression and tyranny. It was because of their lawlessness that the cattlemen could feel justified in everything they did to us: scattering our stock to the four winds, seizing and selling it at market, or killing it outright and leaving it to rot.

Our men *had* to band together out of personal safety and protection of the hoofed assets—it simply wasn't safe to ride the range alone by 1889.

Solidarity *was* imperative.

During the year following Jack's conversation with Burgee, our home became a convention hall where the men organized the resistance. Hearing their discussions gave me a marvelous opportunity to watch them and decipher what truly made them tick. They were men worth knowing.

The change in Burgee was astounding. He was affable, showed genuine leadership capabilities and was pleasantly sober. Jack said, "All he needed was to know he was valued and be included in the plan." And he proved worthy of the inclusion in the long run. In addition to Will Standifer, Whit Fielder, and the Boot Five's Lattis and Shaw, the Johnson brothers came on occasion. Sometimes Allison was there, but as time went by he seemed to slip further and further into his occluded silences.

This core group, which represented the best and brightest of the independents—or Rustlers, as they increasingly called themselves with pride—decided on proper range conduct, discussed strategies for resisting the unconstitutional laws, disseminated information on known white cap activities, and generally set the example for others to follow. Their little organization was nothing sophisticated—these were highly independent, uncomplicated men. But their decisions were efficient and intelligent.

They agreed on everything but the maverick issue, and Jack was the only dissenter there. The lawyer in him found it difficult to accept the act of mavericking, an outlawed practice, as essential to our resistance. But in truth it was the very crux of the issue. Will Standifer, though generally a man of few words, explained the Rustlers' philosophy in a way even a lawyer could understand.

"Before you came here, Jack, before the killer winter brought disaster to the cow business, the big outfits set the price on mavericks at five dollars a head to their hands. That's a pretty shiny enticement to a man who makes thirty dollars a month. If he's a top hand, he don't have trouble findin' fifteen mavericks a month in good weather, and he might make nine hundred dollars in a year. That's a lot of money.

"There might be several reasons a man decides to work for himself. Maybe he's worked for one too many knot-headed bosses. Maybe he don't like to answer to another man. It's something cowboys always dream of, but few have the gumption to try, because it's a scary thing to go out on your own. You won't have a bunkhouse or hot grub waitin' at the end of a hard day. And you sure ain't gonna make nine hundred dollars workin' for yourself until you've built a good herd, and that might take years."

"Shoot, around here it could take forever," said Ben Lattis, "since the big fellas won't let you market your stock—and can even steal it from you outright."

"Good point," Will concurred. "So, you see, anybody who says we went into business because we're a lazy bunch of so-and-so's has no idea how much work it is to gather and brand range stock. And they don't know the hardships we're willin' to endure. You know there's a principal at work here, Jack, and everyone in this room has staked his life on it."

The men all nodded in agreement.

"You see," Will continued, "as long as we were brandin' mavericks for the big outfits everything was just fine. But the minute one independent branded one for himself, he became an outlaw. Why? By what right can the Association claim every stray in this Territory? They're not the only people who own cattle in Wyoming—I own some, you all own some, there's dozens of small ranchers here. What makes it alright for *them* but not for us? That's the same as a man sayin' 'There's a field of wild strawberries over yonder. I'll pay you to go pick me a bucket of 'em. But if you eat so much as *one*, mister, I'll hang your hide.' He's tellin' you that you can't have at any price what he can have for free. That's a man who'll claim strawberries today, mavericks tomorrow—and next week, fellas, he'll be claimin' you and me."

"Be a cold day in hell before anyone of them owns me," said Ben. "Beg your pardon, Josie."

"The problem is," said Jack, "they consider it their stock to begin with. They feel, by reason of their majority ownership on the range, the mavericks belong to them."

"The majority rules—is that it?" said Billy. "My granddad always told me majority rule sounded a little too much like mob law. Guess he was right, boys."

"What I don't like is their arrogant high-handedness," said Burgee. "They're saying we can't own cattle and we can't join their club."

"Who'd want to," grumbled Ben.

"To hear the cattlemen tell it," inserted Whit wryly, "only associated heifers have the gift of reproduction."

General laughter greeted the comment.

"That's comical, isn't it?" nodded Burgee. "What's not comical is their ability to manufacture laws that assume it to be a fact. That does to *us* what they're symbolically doing to our heifers. Think about that one, fellas. They're saying that their size, money, and power give them the right, not only to ownership of every maverick on the range, but to take what is ours—up to and including our lives."

"I ain't in the habit of usin' fifty dollar words like tyranny, Jack," said Will, "but I know what it means. And I know the founders of this nation outlawed it a hundred years ago. So when you boil this down to the fundamentals, what we're doin' with this maverick issue is defendin' the Constitution. And we're willin' to risk everything to do it."

Jack nodded, thinking. "I can certainly understand your views, and I won't attempt to dissuade you all from what you're doing. It's a brave undertaking. I just hope you respect my position on this—while the Maverick Laws are on the books, no mavericks will ever wear the JS Quarter Circle."

"That's your choice, Jack," said Will. "Of course we'll respect it."

The others concurred.

"I agree wholeheartedly that it's unconstitutional and it must be changed," Jack continued. "But if you boys are set on challenging the law in this fashion, there are some ground rules that need to be established and followed so it's fully apparent to the lawmakers in this Territory that they've been put on notice."

When the lawyer in Jack spoke, he had the group's undivided attention.

"I know this goes without saying in the present company, but only full-grown stock could be deemed astray and not owned, so only full mavericks can be branded. And this branding needs to be done in groups, for the sake of safety *and* to afford witnesses. I don't want any of you riding alone, you hear?" He looked at Allison, though he knew his words were useless.

"And if you're really set on this course," he said finally, "the branding should be done in the presence of Association reps, because that's the only way you will openly challenge these laws."

"Well, Jack," Ben said finally, "I hardly find it practical to go round-up a rep just to get my work done. Any man interested in turnin' a profit don't have time to run all over Creation, you know."

"And just how much in profits have you turned lately, Ben?" Jack said. "When was the last time anybody in this room was able to ship cattle to market?"

"Sounds to me," said Whit, "like that last stipulation might have to wait for the right set of circumstances, Jack."

Most of what Jack was requiring already was being practiced by the group. I explained earlier the cowboy rite of passage in mavericking only full- grown stuff—these men would have considered it an insult in the first degree to try and pass a suckling calf off as a maverick. And with the exception of Allison, they were already working in twos or threes for the sake of protection. But so far Allison was the only one who had had the audacity to brand in front of Association reps.

No one said as much that night, but such audacity also required an enormous amount of courage—or in Allison's case, an enormous lack of fear. It's one thing to challenge an adversary by covert acts, it's quite another to make that challenge head-on, especially when you're a handful of men going head-on with a big group in open country. For in truth, the only way the law would be challenged *openly* would be to brand mavericks where there were plenty of witnesses *on both sides*. This would require the branding to be done in front of reps within the framework of the Association's scheduled round-ups. And that was impossible—our men were blackballed from round-up.

But the time would come when this courageous feat would be accomplished anyway.

CHAPTER FOUR
1891
(Excerpt from the journal of Josie Watson Stewart)

*J*une 25, 1891 - Horrible news came our way today. A horse rancher who has been missing for two weeks was found a mile from his home, hanging in a gulch. Who are these men who can take a father from his supper table and discard him in a gully with no concern for his life or those of the spouse and children left behind? When I hear these things fear shoots through me like a stab of warning from the Grim Reaper, telling me that my family could be next. And I want to snatch my children and husband and run away as fast and far as I can go. If ever I thought standing on a principle was righteous and joyful work, let me be reminded of this day. It may appear righteous and joyful to untried eyes from the perspective of time and distance, but it is a windstorm of raw fear in the here and now. Each day that passes the terror goes deeper. I feel suffocated by it. Only the anger saves me, the rage at the injustice of it all. That's what keeps me going, indeed what keeps me sane.

July 29, 1891 - I can hardly believe what has happened! It's abominable enough that the men who lynched the horse rancher, a deputy U.S. Marshal and a stock detective, have admitted to the atrocity with glib arrogance and gotten off with no more than a reprimand. But the fact that one of them has been appointed executor of the dead man's estate is beyond my comprehension! Am I so naïve? I thought this sort of thing only happened during the Dark Ages, the Inquisition, or in obscure countries ruled by military dictatorships. The framers of our Constitution are surely rolling over in their graves like whirlwinds.

The mind is a truly remarkable gadget. Fear sharpens it. And if fear and terror are present on an extended basis, the mind dulls the edges of the terror, growing inured, even while it hones its alertness with the fear.

I cannot describe what it was like to live in those times in that place. To say that it was a character-builder would understate the situation entirely. It was not something I would ever wish to relive, though I must admit that if one could overlook the terror and violence it *was* intellectually stimulating—the act of rising to a just cause, the conscious effort of holding onto a principle. My memory of those days is far better than my memory of the more mundane parts of my life—it's all in there, imprinted on my mind as if burned by a brand.

But brands are, after all, scar tissue.

It is impossible to overlook the violence.

"Why would they hang a horse rancher, Jack?" I asked in baffled horror. "He wasn't rustling mavericks—he didn't even own cattle!"

"Apparently, when they came to his home," Jack told me, "they had a warrant that accused him of buying horses stolen from an associated cattle outfit. According to the wife, he went with them gladly. He insisted then and there that he was not a buyer of stolen stock, and he'd march right into town with them to prove it. All I can say is, if they thought their case was strong enough, they would have brought him in on that warrant to see him hanged legally."

I threw up my hands helplessly. "What is going on here?"

"A war, Josie—pure and simple. And they have every intention of winning it by this first-strike campaign of terror."

In a way, the lynching of the horse rancher achieved the opposite effect of what the cattlemen were aiming for. Certainly, it sparked the raw fear once again, that gnawing terror that went so deep it became something physical in the knowledge that it could easily happen to you. But it also sparked an anger, deeper even than the fear, which cemented our solidarity.

In the case of Will Standifer, the anger completely annihilated the fear—if the man ever possessed any. He had been thoroughly incensed by the lynching of the woman two years earlier, then at spring round-up of '91 ten of his heifers were seized.

Understand that, for all his philosophizing on the maverick issue, in practice Will kept pretty much to Jack's ideas on mavericking. He had come out of the hard winter with money in his pocket not only because he made the wages of a wagon boss and was adept at rustling mavericks for his employer, but because he was frugal. A rarity among men of his profession, Will was not given to binges of drinking and womanizing with his wages. He bought cattle instead. By '91 he had two hundred head on the range and a pocketful of bills of sale. When his heifers were taken, he fell into a solemn decisive anger. The lynching of the horse rancher was the last straw.

All that summer of '91 it seemed he was determined to provoke the cattlemen. He followed every wagon of every big outfit that came into our country and made a deliberate show of checking anything they rounded up. He wasn't about to allow one head of our stock to be stolen, and he wanted those cattlemen to understand that he knew who the *real* brigands were. They could talk themselves blue in the face from one end of this nation to the other, write unconstitutional laws for their own benefit and yell "Thief!" as loud as their formidable voices could shout. But they would never intimidate Will Standifer. And by the fall of 1891 they knew it as surely as they knew the sun would rise.

Something about this one-man-stand reached a key in Allison. For over a year he had been slipping into darker silences, drinking heavily, riding alone, taking more foolhardy chances than ever with his roping—and even preferring the company of his horses over that of friends or even his cow-chip courtesans. In the summer of '91 it all came crashing in around him. It was bound to happen sometime. He had a jerk-down accident. The steer Allison was roping took a sudden leaping shift that caught the horse off guard and jerked him down.

When Jack and Will brought Allison into the house and laid

him on the table, I thought he was dead. His shirt was soaked in blood and his skin was a ghastly gray—not a color associated with life at all. My first notion was that he had been yet another victim of the cattle war and I froze, hand on my mouth.

"What happened?" I asked, running for the medicine box.

"Jerked down," said Will, tearing at Allison's shirt. "Horse landed right on his chest. Saddle horn barely missed his heart."

Jerked down. Well, that was something normal to range work. My horror gave way to practicality. "Mart, put some water on to boil and fill the buckets with the coldest water you can pull from the creek. Find a nice shady spot."

Little Henry stared, entranced by the scene around the table. "Whassa madda wiff Unca Ally?"

"He had a horse wreck, honey. He's hurt bad and Mama has to help him. Dudley, please take the little ones outside."

The cabin was a sudden flurry of motion as I rummaged through the medicines, the men stripped away Allison's clothes, and Dudley tried shooing the fascinated children toward the door even as he too was compelled to stare at the wreckage. Mart was the only exception to the panic and awe. He never spilled a drop of that water. Even at such a tender age in such a circumstance he was the calmest of souls.

What I heard from the table chilled me—the sound of a punctured lung. Blood flew from Allison's mouth as his torso bolted upright with a wracking cough. My eyes met Jack's. Both of us knew we were standing over a dying man, yet Jack's eyes pleaded with me so. I had had plenty of nursing experience from helping my father.

"Lift his shoulders, Will," I said, stuffing pillows underneath. "We have to keep his chest elevated."

In addition to the crushed chest, his face, arms and legs were a battlefield of lacerations, rope burns and embedded gravel. The three of us worked on him until midnight, exchanging cold packs on the swelling, cleansing wounds, stitching them, salving, plucking dirt and gravel from his tortured limbs. I never expected he would survive the night. But he did.

We made a bed for him by the stove, kept his shoulders elevated, and watched him drift in and out of consciousness for days. He must have been in a world of fiery pain, but he never cried out, never whimpered even in his sleep. I have to say, Martin Allison Stewart was the toughest man I ever knew.

And I will admit also that his illness showed me that he was as loved by his peers as Jack—if not more so. Cowboys came to his sickbed from as far away as eighty miles and more. Every day for weeks there was at least one, sometimes three or four. It occurred to me, watching this parade of disciples, that if Allison's wounds *had* been inflicted by the cattlemen, the war would have started right then in earnest. And we probably would have won.

I know it embarrassed him when he finally regained his faculties, to find himself beholden to me. I could tell by the look in his eyes that he felt himself unworthy of my constant attentions. If he could have gotten up, I'm sure he would have bolted out that door the minute his eyes focused. As it was, he lay there in silent pain, coughing stridently.

I probably could have been nicer to him. I wasn't mean, mind you. I wasn't anything. I put my feelings for Allison away. Under the circumstances, I thought it was the only courteous thing to do. I was neither pleasant nor rude, neither kind nor mean. But what he perceived was something worse than disdain. He saw indifference. I didn't intend to convey that.

Luckily for his sake, the children loved him and hovered about, making certain there was always water in his cup, that he had something to nibble on if he wanted it. He was good with them; I will say that for Ally. He probably felt it his duty to keep them entertained, since it was all he could do in his crippled state. He would tell them range stories about wild longhorn cattle, about bears and snakes and horses. Insatiable, they would bring him books and he would try to read to them, but they ultimately ended up reading to him instead. That, too, embarrassed him.

It was the cowboys who came to visit who told us the stories of Will Standifer's one-man war with the big outfits. From the first story, Allison showed visible improvement, and with each successive story grew better, as if he had finally found something worth living for. Even though he was not yet healed and would forever thereafter live on one lung and a caved-in chest, he left as soon as he could ride and hooked up with Will.

The rise to a challenge must have been what Allison needed to regain his health, and perhaps even retrieve something of his long-lost self-respect. He dedicated himself completely to Will's campaign, foregoing his usual depravities. That summer of '91 nobody stared cross-eyed at the two of them—they were really going rough, pointedly looking over the shoulders of the big outfits in open provocation. They were ready to fight anybody. But it was at fall round-up that they made their boldest move.

In those days of open range when round-up wagons worked a region, any mavericks found would be branded for the owners of the wagons. We didn't have the resources to fund wagons and were, of course, blackballed from officially participating in round-up. But our fellows worked with pack outfits and by Jack's recommendation and Will's determined example had, by the fall of '91, gotten to where they would work right alongside some of the round-up wagons that came through our country. They knew most of the cowhands on the round-up circle and things went along fairly smoothly as long as each side stuck to branding their own stock. They did virtually everything together, except divvy up the mavericks evenly. The mavericks were always cut out and branded for the Associated wagons.

In the fall of '91 Will, Allison and the Boot Five partners were working alongside the Bar C wagon up Buffalo creek. When they got the cattle gathered and the round-up boss cut out the mavericks for the Bar C, Will stopped him.

"There's more'n one outfit here, Hank," he said.

"What're you aimin' at, Will?"

"Fairness. By rights, your outfit should only get a quarter of those mavericks. A quarter should go to the Boot Five and a quarter each to Allison and me," Will stated.

"I can't do that, and you know it. Fair or not, I have to abide by the law."

"Well, Hank, I don't happen to believe that a bad law is better than none at all," Will said. "And since you big outfits've been takin' everything on the range for a matter of years now—includin' stuff that lawfully belongs to us—I believe we'll start to even things up right here and put *all* these mavericks in the Rustler cut. I personally am claiming ten for the heifers that were stolen from me last spring."

And he proceeded to do just that while Allison and the Boot Five boys stood the others off.

Hank was fit to be tied. But he couldn't stop it from happening. Of the crew he had, there were only two who might be considered fighting men. Whit Fielder was to say years later, "Will was the nerviest man I ever met. He really had the best of it that time."

The range may have been as big and unpopulated as an ocean, but word traveled quicker than one might imagine. And news of the maverick branding incident spread across that country like wildfire. We could only guess what effect it had in the halls of power at the stock association, but undoubtedly it caused violent shock waves and sputtering fury.

It acted on the little outfits like a tonic. We felt empowered, finally. And what the reps of the big outfits faced on the range for the rest of that season must have made them feel nothing short of impotent.

Years later, Joe Rankin, who went on to become a United States Marshal, would tell the story of what it was like on the range that fall. At the time Joe was repping for the Cross H, on circle, gathering stock in the round-up. He had some cattle together and got over a hill ahead of the end of the bunch. When he looked back, the tail of the herd was missing. Puzzled, he rode back and discovered three men hazing the cattle down a draw.

"Say!" he hailed them. "Where you takin' those cattle? I'm repping for the Cross H and there's Cross H cattle in that bunch. Don't you boys think we should take all this stuff to the round-up?"

They looked at one another. They knew Joe to be a decent fellow, and they agreed. When they got to round-up, Joe told George Melvin, the round-up boss, what had happened.

"Alright, let's stop this," Melvin said.

"How?" asked Rankin.

"We'll just kick these fellas out of round-up and be done with it."

"Okay. But who you gonna get to help us, George?"

"Why, there's several fellas."

"Name them," said Joe.

Sentiment was running high for the little outfits. Most of the working hands on the range were cheering us on. When it came to a count, Melvin could only think of three in the round-up who weren't questionable.

Two days later the same thing happened to Rankin again. This time the men stood their ground. "There's not a Cross H cow in this bunch, Joe, so ride on." And Joe rode on.

To give a full idea of the situation, I must recount a companion story Rankin told about the atmosphere on the range at that time. During the same round-up, just days later, Melvin told Rankin several of his Cross H horses had gotten out of the cavvy and were last seen headed toward the home ranch. So Joe struck out and found them. He had the herd in a dog trot along the bottom of a draw a mile from round-up when the lead horses suddenly spooked, sending the whole bunch into a scatter over the hills up either side of the draw. With instant caution, Joe reined in, drew his rifle and waited to see what had scared them. After a few minutes of silence, Joe went carefully up the draw where he discovered five baby calves tied down with little bits of rope. He got out his pocket knife and cut them loose, then gathered his horses and rode on to round-up. He told Melvin about it.

"Undoubtedly," Joe added, "somebody'll be going back up there to brand those calves."

Sure enough, along came Jed Argand. "Lost my slicker back yonder," he said to Melvin. "I was a little busy bringin' in a bunch of cattle at the time, but I believe I'll ride back and get it now."

Melvin and Rankin looked at one another as he rode off.

"There goes a thief," said Melvin. And he was right.

Argand was a man of the variety I called border lopers—and of a ruthless stripe. The fact that he was illegally branding suckling calves is sufficient evidence of his character. And this incident shows how the words 'rustler' and 'thief' became irreversibly linked, and why the cattlemen equated men of his ilk with our side of the war. In my opinion, Jed Argand wasn't much different than Ed Weston or Tom Horn. Except he wasn't as smart.

Rankin's stories show what was happening that fall, and quite spontaneously. But it wasn't just Will's bold maverick branding foray that sparked this chorus of civil disobedience. People had simply come to the end of their tolerance with the tyranny.

Yet another spontaneous reaction erupted among the settlers. Though it was something Jack and I could not condone, neither could we blame people for surrendering to it. As Whit Fielder later explained, "Some of these little fellas around here who would never have beefed a steer figured, 'Well, these big fellas are killin' off people and seizin' our stuff or killin' it. So we'll just even up with 'em.' And they started killin' beef."

These were people who had been pushed too far. Some were down to their last nickel, or worse, and rather than see their families starve for lack of being able to market their own beef, they felt as justified in taking the cattlemen's beef as the cattlemen did in seizing our stock. Settlers had subsisted on wild game for so long it was becoming scarce, while the cattlemen's herds continued to proliferate. When associated beef began making its way to some settler's tables, it was referred to sardonically as Slow Elk.

This only made the range tensions worse. The air was thick with a hostility and discord you could have cut with a knife. I fully expected an armed conflict to erupt at any moment. Our men were never without loaded weapons by then, even in sleep, and lived in constant anticipation of ambush. In the throes of a nightmare, Billy Shaw shot several holes through the bunkhouse of the Boot Five dreaming he was under attack. It took Ben Lattis and two hired hands to bring him out of the nightmare without harming someone.

By the late fall of 1891, many independents found they couldn't handle the tension anymore and an exodus began. We had a handful of these men approach us. Jumbo MacKenzie was the first. As his nickname infers, he was a giant of a man and certainly not the sort who scared easily. But Jumbo was newly married, and I didn't blame him for decamping.

I didn't blame any of them.

They were men who had maybe twenty head of cattle on the range. They didn't want to get hung or shot, and for a little piece of traveling money and a horse, they wanted to get out. Jack certainly understood their trepidation and offered them money on loan, but he was hesitant to start buying stock that may have been mavericked.

But the Boot Five partners and Whit Fielder weren't. Whit traded as little as a saddle horse for a bunch of cattle. Billy Shaw said they kept themselves strapped all the time bailing those men out—because we were still unable to sell at market.

The only outlet the small ranchers had in the area was a slaughterhouse owned by a man whose sentiments were with us. He had a contract with the army to provide beef to Fort McKinney, and he would take our stuff at five dollars a head, which was half of market value. But it was better than nothing. Unfortunately, there was a limit to how many head he could take, so it wasn't much of an outlet.

The cattlemen decried him for buying what they considered stolen stuff. And they claimed the Boot Five's eight hundred were stolen as well and used Lattis and Shaw as an example of the "enormous depredations" accusation, inferring that they had mavericked the entire herd. After Will's branding incident and the rash of civil disobedience at round-up, they knew they had a range-wide rebellion on their hands. Something hand to be done to quell it.

In the early morning hours of November first, three armed men broke through the door of the cabin Will Standifer was leasing. "We've got you now, you son of a bitch," one said.

Will rolled off the bed firing, as the three in the doorway tried to obliterate him. They succeeded in assassinating the pillow. In a close room full of feathers and gun smoke, no one could see a thing. All they knew was that Standifer was not dead and he was backing them out the door with rapid gunfire. One was hit and they all made a quick retreat, leaving a new Winchester leaning against the doorjamb in their haste.

Will found the initials E.W. engraved on the stock of the carbine.

Tommy Case, a fourteen year old ranch hand at the Bar C, had just finished milking the cow at dawn when he turned to find a man standing not three feet behind him. Tommy was so scared he dropped the milk bucket. It was Will.

"Who's here, Tommy?" said Will.

" J—just me, sir."

"Who was here last night?"

"Mr. Finn, the ranch foreman."

"Where is he now?"

"I dunno. He was gone when I got up."

Will left as quietly as he had come.

He showed up at our door, his horse in a lather, little more than an hour later. By that time the measure of the incident had had time to sink in and he was visibly shaken. Jack was furious when he heard the story. And when Will showed him the Winchester, he was ready to go finish the whole conflict then and there.

"Weston! I should have hung that SOB in Texas! He's got to be stopped, that's all there is to it."

"Calm down, Jack," said Will. "We gotta think this thing through."

"The time for thinking is over. They started it. And by the gods, we've got every right to defend ourselves. It's a miracle you're alive, Will."

"I'm a light sleeper. I heard 'em before they threw open the door."

"But what if you hadn't? They intended to murder you!"

I touched Jack's arm. "But they didn't succeed. That's what counts."

Fear gave me an odd serenity that morning. I was five months into expecting our fourth child, and the louder and more agitated Jack became, the more serene I grew to counterbalance him. Will sounded more like the attorney.

"Josie's right," he said. "Now sit down so we can discuss this thing. We gotta do something, but we better do it right or more of this dry-gulchin' and ambushin' will follow."

Once he was thinking clearly, the lawyer in Jack held forth. He ultimately decided that in the absence of having the right to simply shoot Weston on sight, sending him to jail was the next best thing. They needed a positive identification of the perpetrators so they could file a charge of attempted murder.

"Finn knows something," said Will. "Whether he was in on it or not, I couldn't say. But he knows something."

"Let's go have a little chat with him," said Jack.

They found Finn alone on a trail above the Bar C and cornered him. He was nervous at seeing Will. They demanded to know who was involved in the ambush. Scared, Finn blurted out a confession. He had only guarded the horses, he contended. It was Weston and the other two men who ambushed Will.

"Name them," demanded Jack.

"I only know one of 'em—name's Elliot."

Will looked at Jack. "He was one of the men who hung that horse rancher."

"Hey, I got nothin' against you, Will," Finn insisted. "You know that. Hell, we worked together as friends for years. I was just showin' these birds where you lived."

"That's an awful strange way of exhibiting friendship," Jack pointed out.

"I didn't know what they was up to! Hell, they said they only wanted to talk to him!"

"Do you honestly expect us to believe that?"

"I don't care what you believe. That's what they said."

Jack scrutinized him. "What did you expect three assassins to converse with Will about in the middle of the night, Mike?"

"How should I know?"

"I notice you didn't deny they were assassins. Was it not the Bar C wagon that your boss Hank was running up Buffalo creek a few weeks ago?"

"Yeah, he was up there. So what?"

"Are you going to pretend to be the only man on this range who hasn't heard what Will did up there?"

"Okay, so maybe they was going to scare him a little."

Jack gazed at him forthrightly. "Mike, they broke through the door and fired on a sleeping man. Don't you think he might have ended up just a little too dead to be scared?"

"What're you tryin' to get from me, Stewart?"

"The truth."

"I've said all I'm gonna say."

"I don't think so. You're an accessory to attempted murder, Mike. We're willing to let you extricate yourself from this mess by cooperating with us. Or you will be named in the charge. Which will it be?"

"You got the information you wanted. For chrissake, can't you just leave it at that?"

"I'm afraid not. You just made a confession, witnessed by two people. Now make your choice."

Finn said nothing, cornered and angry.

"Leave him be," said Will, to Jack's utter surprise. "Go home, Mike. Just be damn careful who you side with from now on. And that's a direct warning—the only one you'll get."

Finn wasted no time departing.

When he was out of sight, Jack turned to Will. "Are you out of your mind?" he fumed. "That man tried to kill you, and you just let him ride away!"

"He was only being loyal to his outfit, Jack. And he didn't take part in the ambush. He told us what we needed to know, and for that I'm willin' to let him go with a warning."

"Your forgiving attitude might be well-and-good under normal circumstances, but we're in the middle of a range war. Right now, all it does is weaken your case. Damn it, Will—we needed that man as a witness!"

"He'd never testify for us. I guarantee it."

"Well, he won't now, that's certain!"

"We got enough to file a charge. That'll do for now."

The county seat was over sixty miles away, and Jack insisted they get themselves in there and talk to the sheriff before Weston decided to make another surprise visit in the night. They stopped at home only long enough to tell me what they were doing and to eat. By then I had lost my serenity. The range war was on the threshold of my home, and I was getting touchy as a teased snake. Jack insisted that Allison stay with me until he returned from town.

"I can take care of myself, Jack. You know how I feel about your brother. And given what happened to Will, I'm sure I'd be safer without him. Undoubtedly they're after Allison, too."

"Josie, please! Don't argue with me, that's all I ask. I will not leave you alone in your condition."

"Burgees are right next door. They'll watch out for me. Take Allison or send him away, Jack. I don't want him here!"

"He's staying, and that's final," Jack said sternly, and walked out.

He didn't kiss me good-bye or even squeeze my hand. He just grabbed his hat, strode to his horse and mounted. I was more stunned by this lapse of affection than his curtly-delivered directive.

Will must have noticed. He finished his last bite of biscuit and stood from the table, taking his hat from a peg on the wall as he came toward me.

"Thanks for the food," he said gently.

I was staring out the door after Jack and something in my look must have seemed stricken and plaintive to Will.

"Don't worry," he said. "I'll bring him home safe."

I looked at him, this man who was so much a part of our lives, closer than a brother, the only devoted friend besides my husband

I could lay claim to on earth. I grabbed his hand and squeezed it before he could walk away.

"Bring yourself home safe too, Will."

He smiled. "Aw, don't fret over me. I got nine lives."

"It's the fact that you've used up eight-and-a-half of them that worries me," I said.

I didn't allow myself to wonder how I could live without them. Oddly enough, when death is right outside your door you don't think of dying. You think obsessively of carrying on the business of life.

Perhaps Jack was right in insisting Allison should stay. My ire for the man kept me from worrying every minute about the dangers of their trip to town.

CHAPTER FIVE
WINTER
(Excerpt from the Journal of Josie Watson Stewart)

November 15, 1891 - Finally the settlers have organized. Prompted by the news of the ambush on Will Standifer, a meeting was held three days ago, which was attended by virtually every small rancher and farmer in the county—over two hundred people. I even defied convention and attended in my condition; we felt it important that whole families came. We are now, formally, the Northern Plains Farmers and Livestock Growers Association. Reporters from three regional newspapers were invited to attend in hopes that publication of our plight reaches the outside and justice may be served with the eyes of the nation on us. One reporter assured us that he would get the story to a Denver paper.

November 22, 1891 - Instead of making things better, I am beginning to think our organizing has made things worse. Somehow our story has never reached the outside, and tempers on both sides of the range war have come to a volatile state. Arguments and even fisticuffs are a daily affair when one of our men crosses paths with a rep from a big outfit. Jack lives on the edge of sanity and talks of nothing but war and Weston. I have hidden the rifle for fear that he will start the conflict himself. I know it's a useless gesture since he is never without his loaded pistol, carrying it even to the privy as if it were part of his anatomy. What kind of world are we bringing yet another child into? I fear gravely for our future.

The emotional side of pregnancy is difficult enough to control without having a range war on your porch to complicate matters. And Jack—he was like a madman those last days of November.

The trip to town to file charges had ended in frustration for him. Will was too honest. Instead of specifically identifying Weston, Will reported the ambush exactly as it happened, obscuring smoke and all, and recounted the conversation with Finn, naming him as the source of identification. This gave Finn a chance to recant and Weston the opportunity to produce an alibi, which both did. So the report went into the files as an unsolved assault with no charges of record.

Jack was furious.

At every mention of the incident he ranted at Will, who was staying with us then. Will remained unflappable in the face of Jack's ire. Had their friendship been less than it was, Jack may well have pushed Will beyond sufferance. But Will was the most tolerant man I ever met, and plainly honest. He had told the truth, he said, that was the best any man could do.

"There's such a thing as too much truth, Will," Jack grumbled. "Do you think the truth amounts to a hill of beans to Weston?"

"I ain't Weston," Will pointed out.

"No, but if we're going to fight this thing and win, we have to use the law to trip them. What do you think they're doing? They'll abuse any law to get what they want, or manufacture new ones if it suits them."

"Almost sounds like you're asking me to use their own underhanded means to whip them, Jack. And you know I can't do that."

I don't know how many times this conversation was repeated; the words changed but the gist was the same. Whenever Jack thought about the report he angrily brought it up, and each time Will deftly ended the conversation by standing firmly on the truth. Then I would hear it again at night in the privacy of our bedchamber, where Jack would carry on about it some more.

What could I say? Personally, I sided with Will, though I tried to understand Jack's perspective. Lawyers sometimes live in a different world, I guess—a place where the law is an ambiguous art, pliable like clay. But truth is truth—fixed, not malleable. At least it is to me. So I said nothing. I listened to him, lonesome in my fears, without even a chance at solace from my distracted husband.

As the month wore on and the settler organization only seemed to provoke greater aggression from the cattlemen, Jack fell into an eerie silence, his fixation on Weston having taken on the ominous characteristic of obsession. When the time came for his yearly trip to town to buy winter supplies, I got worried. Weston would be in town. I took Will aside and we talked. He was worried too.

"Go with him, Will," I insisted.

"And leave you here alone? If something happened I'd never forgive myself, not to mention what Jack would do to me."

"Ally will be here. And Burgees are right next door. I'll be fine."

Imagine me finding a useful excuse to have Allison stay.

Will smiled knowingly. "I thought you didn't like Ally loafing around here," he said. "Are you sure you wouldn't rather send him with Jack?"

"Heavens no! He'd use Jack's mood to incite a riot."

"I can't just invite myself along, Josie. He'll know something's up."

"But he's less likely to do something rash if you're with him, Will. Please go. Please!"

He braced my shoulder reassuringly. "Alright. I'll head toward town later this morning. That way I'll be there when he heads off tomorrow."

That was the day I hid the rifle. It was a silly thing to do—more symbolic than anything. Even in his obsession, Jack would never have taken the rifle and left me unarmed.

The next morning as he was preparing the wagon for the trip, I fixed him a big breakfast. The children were still sleeping as he came in. It was dark outside yet. His calm was an abrupt departure from the previous days of anxious brooding. He took my hand and gently drew me close.

"I want to apologize for my behavior lately," he said. "I know you're worried, and I want to assure you that I'm fine now."

His composure gave me incentive to speak freely. "I can't help but worry, Jack, the way you've been going on about Weston."

"I know. And I'm sorry." He stroked my hair. "You were right and so was Will. Truth is always the best road to take. I've been stalling, I guess, expecting someone to save me from having to tell the truth about Weston. And I've finally realized I have to face this thing."

"What do you mean? Are you going to turn him in?"

He nodded. "I have to."

My heart raced. I was proud of him for coming to this conclusion, of course, but I was now more scared than ever. I sensed something ominous. "Do you have to do it now?" I asked.

"Yes. Before he has had a chance to kill again."

I took a breath. "How will you do it?"

"I'll confront him in a crowded place, make a public revelation of his identity, and have him arrested."

"Oh, Jack, that sounds so dangerous."

"Actually, it's the safest way to do it, Josie. He's a man who works covertly. Confronting him in a crowd is the best thing. He'll go without a fight, knowing the burden of proof rests on my shoulders. I am, after all, going to have to prove that he is *not* Ed Weston. And I may not succeed. But at least I'll have made every effort to put him away and do some damage to his credibility in this community."

I didn't know what to do, what to say. At that moment I loved him so deeply no words could convey what I felt. So I gathered him in an embrace that went straight to the soul.

"I love you, Josephine," he said.

I began to cry then. The only other time he had ever called me by my full name was during our wedding ceremony. I wanted to just hold him there, keep him from going. Keep him safe. If I could have spoken, I would have begged him not to leave. But there was a lump in my throat the size of Omaha.

I don't know how Mart always knew when I was in an emotional state, but suddenly he was there joining the hug, his little arms around our waists, assuring both of us that everything was fine. Somehow my eldest son had, by the age of five, decided it was his destiny in life to be his mother's protector.

A trip to town for supplies might take a week or more. Roads were rough and meandered around, over and through flats, creeks, and draws. Wagons moved slowly. I didn't expect Jack home before December second or third.

All that last week of November I kept myself too busy to worry. When the chores were done I gathered the children around for extra lessons and study. They all complained at this, feeling educationally abused. That spring we had formed a school district in the valley and elected John Burgee school teacher, so they felt putting in their four months with him was enough for one year. But I had to keep my mind off what may be happening in town or I would surely have gone insane. So school reconvened at the kitchen table.

Ally was a help, I will grant him that. He sensed the reason for my busy compulsion and made a useful presence of himself. I even think he learned a few things at the kitchen school.

December third was a blustery day. The cold wind felt good on my face as I stepped onto the porch for relief from the hot kitchen. It was bread-baking day.

Foresight is a strange thing. When you sense innately that something is amiss, your mind often overlooks the obvious and denies its own capacity to see a coming catastrophe. I didn't wonder why the men were riding up without Jack, why they hadn't slowed their horseback pace to accommodate his wagon. What struck me first was the way Will sat in his saddle as he rode into the yard with Whit Fielder and Billy Shaw. Though he sat erect, he looked wounded somehow.

Whit and Billy touched their hats somberly in my direction, then went toward Allison at the stable. This too struck me as odd. By then Will had dismounted, walked straight to the porch, and without preamble shocked me silly by surrounding me gently with his arms. It was not a lover's embrace; I felt vaguely as if I were holding him up. He spoke in my ear and I knew then the reason for the embrace. It was meant to hold me up.

"Jack's dead," he said softly.

I inhaled a sudden chestful of air that wouldn't come back out. It burned like hot glue in my windpipe. Will's arms responded, held me tighter, though he was choked up as well.

I wanted to cry and scream. I had to wake up. This was a bad dream, a horrible nightmare. If I could just scream, I would wake myself up—please—wake up, Josie!

But Will's tears were real on my forehead, the cold wind turning them to traces of hot ice on my cheeks. Beyond his shoulder I saw Whit and Billy, barely able to contain Allison by the corral; heard an inhuman wail come out of Jack's brother like the roar of a wounded grizzly.

And then I knew for certain. This was no dream.

I couldn't say how long we stood there on the porch holding each other up. Time was suspended. From the moment I heard those awful words until somewhere around nine that evening, my life is an unmerciful blur. All I know is that I did not cry. I don't remember how I found the strength or presence of mind to tell the children, or even what I said to them. But I remember Will putting us all down for a nap. I didn't sleep. I lay there seething. The terror was gone. When the worst has happened, all the fear dissipates and what is left in its wake is a decisive, serene anger.

I would never fear them again.

Will cooked supper, though no one could muster an appetite. After the children were sleeping and Whit and Billy had control of Allison in the stable, I seated myself across from Will at the kitchen table.

"Tell me," I demanded.

I know he thought I blamed him. After all, I had begged him to go with Jack and protect him from this very disaster. Perhaps I did blame him at that moment. He looked so stricken, my eyes must have cut like daggers.

"It's not your fault, Will." I tried to sound less bitter. "Just tell me what happened. I need to know."

He looked at me. "Everything?" he asked.

"Yes, sir. The whole terrible story."

He was reluctant to begin, but my determined stare gave him little choice. "After Jack picked up the supplies," Will said, "he went all over town looking for Weston. Someone must've tipped Weston off, because he was wise enough to avoid Jack."

"How could that be?" I interrupted. "No one knew of Jack's intention to turn him in but me."

Will hesitated. "Actually, that day Jack told me and Whit and Billy what he was planning. He may have told more people."

"That's absurd. You know how close-mouthed he was."

"Ordinarily, yes. But he had been drinking, Josie."

I sat ramrod straight and glared. "I don't believe you."

Will looked apologetic. "You said you wanted to hear everything."

What could have possessed Jack to do that, especially when he had so important a task to accomplish? "Was he drinking with you three?" I probed.

"No, he had been drinking before we ran into him."

"I don't understand that at all."

"He was overwrought, Josie. He had been running around here like a crazy man for a month."

"No." I shook my head vehemently. "The morning he left he was as calm as could be."

"The long ride to town probably gave him too much time to think. I'm sure it didn't help that Weston kept one step ahead of him, either. Anyway, late the afternoon of the thirtieth the three of us convinced him to head for home. It was obvious he wasn't going to catch Weston. By that time he had sobered up and was worried that Weston might try to ambush him on the road, so he bought a shotgun and a dog, thinking the animal might smell trouble . . . and make a nice Christmas present for the children."

He sighed then. "We all thought he was just being jumpy,

that he was still carrying on like he'd been doing all month. But we assured him we'd keep Weston busy if he showed his face. So Jack left and spent the night outside town at the Cross H. The morning of December first he was on the road early. He was only eight miles south of town when it happened. Someone had been waiting for him to cross the bottom of a draw. When he started up the other side, he would be busy with the horses and the assassin would have a clear hit. He was shot in the back, Josie. There was evidence that someone had planned and waited for him."

"Who found him?"

"A man named Charles was headed into town when he heard shots. Came over a rise and found his own neighbor standing in a secluded draw with a smoking gun. The wagon had been led up the draw away from the road, the horses shot in their traces. He killed the dog, too. These were the shots Charles heard."

"So in addition to my husband, I've been criminally deprived of my wagon stock and my children's Christmas present," I observed icily. "Need I ask who Mr. Charles' neighbor is—this man with the smoking gun?"

"You know it was Weston."

"Evidently, he managed to elude you three," I said bitterly.

But Will shook his head. "That's what's unusual. He made a point of being seen all over town that morning."

"How could he be all over town when he was murdering Jack out on the road, Will?" I frowned. "That doesn't make any sense."

"The investigation showed there was about forty minutes between the time the murder took place and Weston was showing himself to the town. A fast horse can make nine miles in that time. And Weston brags on his sorrel's speed every chance he gets."

"Well, well. And there was an eyewitness to place him at the murder site. Does this mean Mr. Weston will in fact be charged with murder?"

"Yes, Josie. Charges have finally been filed."

I rose to my feet, unable to feel even one ounce of vindication.

"It's late, Will. We have a long ride ahead of us tomorrow. We should get some rest."

He stood, concerned. "Do you think you should ride in your condition?"

"Are you suggesting that I miss my husband's funeral?"

"People will understand if you don't come into town. Me and the boys can bring him back here for the burial. It's dangerous for you to ride sixty miles."

"Yes, it is. But we will all go, every last surviving Stewart—including the one yet unborn. Make no mistake, Will. I *want* them to see me in this condition. And I won't bury him in this lonesome little valley where they can forget. I want him buried in town, where his grave will be a constant reminder. It's not just Weston—I hold the entire cattlemen's association accountable for this. They think they can commit murder with impunity. Well, maybe they can contrive to make themselves law-proof in the sanctity of their magnificent halls of power, but when they come home they're still men with families. And this is one family they will be forced to see—a mother with three small children, and a widow-with-child to boot. I want them to understand it *all*, Will. They need to know the ramifications of their lethal arrogance."

The Burgees, bound as well for the funeral, offered to take the children in their wagon. Whit and Billy stayed, ostensibly to take care of the Stewart and Burgee home ranches, but I knew they really stayed to keep Allison contained.

He was a wild man.

I am the last person to advocate the use of alcohol, but in this case it may have been warranted. Whit and Billy kept Allison too drunk to ride, and in Allison's case that required a comatose state. Had he come, he would surely have committed a public murder. He was that rabid.

I rode ahead with Will. The sidesaddle was not uncomfortable in my condition, but I tired easily. It seemed we were stopping every thirty minutes or so to rest. Will was his usual silent self. But I could tell what he was thinking as surely as if I could read his mind. He was castigating himself for being alive while Jack was dead. It was, after all, the ambush on him that put Jack in a tizzy over Weston. I swear I could actually hear his thoughts: Why hadn't he taken Jack more seriously? Why hadn't he found Weston and watched him more closely? Why hadn't he simply rode home with Jack? He was sent to protect, and he had failed. He would never forgive himself.

I reached over finally and touched his arm. "It's not your fault, Will."

"Wish I could believe that," he said.

But my having said it opened a door he assumed had been sealed shut. It was his chance at confession.

"That day," he began, "by the time Jack knew Weston was avoiding him, he wouldn't let us out of his sight. He'd sobered up enough to realize he'd probably opened his head to the wrong person and they'd tipped Weston off. I reckon he also knew that Weston would never be arrested peaceably. I don't think Jack counted on scaring Weston so much, but he knew then that he had. And that's when he knew he was in trouble."

He shook his head helplessly. "If only I had seen it then, Josie, I would never have left him alone for one minute. I failed you. Both of you."

"For heaven's sake, Will, you're not God. I don't expect you to see around corners."

He was silent. After a moment he looked at me. "There's more," he said. "The shotgun. Both barrels had been snapped and the shells never fired."

I stared at him. "What are you trying to tell me?"

"Jack probably saw his assailant. He was expecting it. The first shot at his back glanced off a rivet in his belt. He swung half around, tried to defend himself, but the shells didn't fire. He bought the shotgun and ammunition at a hardware that has known whitecap affiliations. Billy thinks they purposely sold him bum shells."

Bile rose in my throat. With a great force of will I held it back, shook off the rage. If Jack-the-lawyer had taught me one thing, it was to keep your mind on the facts in a crisis. "That's speculative, Will. We have to be careful not to let ourselves get carried away with such notions. Speculation can be our undoing."

"You're right. I'm sorry."

"I'm glad you told me, though."

He was quiet for awhile again, as if priming himself. "There's one more thing," he finally said.

"Oh, Lord, how could there be?"

"I'm sorry."

"No, go ahead. Tell me."

"Later on the same day as Jack's body was brought into town, news came that another murder had taken place."

"Oh, no! Who?"

"Royce Johnson."

"Oh, merciful heaven! That young man never hurt a fly!" I reined in, sick to my stomach. "I have to rest, Will."

Royce Johnson was one of the more polite young men in our circle, one of the brothers I baked bread for who lived two cabins down-valley. He had an unusual talent in the strength of his legs and made a good bronc rider because of it. The others all marveled at his ability to grip a horse. He had been known to break the tree of a saddle on more than one occasion, and had even been offered free ones by saddle-makers who wanted to test their product. If a saddle survived Royce Johnson, it was a well-made piece.

He had gone into town the morning before Jack left to get a load of lumber, flooring for his cabin. He was engaged to be married, and had wanted his bride to have the comfort of a real wood floor.

"I'm sorry for having to tell you all this," said Will. He was standing alongside my horse, arms upheld to assist me in dismounting. "But it's better you know before we get to town."

I let him help me down, painfully near tears. "Why Royce, Will? That boy was never a threat to anyone. He wasn't even a Southern Democrat, for pity's sake."

"I know. He was just a nice kid from Nebraska who had a talent for breaking horses." He took my elbow and walked me around. "They've got it in for us, Josie. We've organized and openly challenged them, and like Jack said, they'll do anything to stop us now. They tried to ambush me. Now they've succeeded with Jack and Royce."

"Jack was murdered because he knew Weston's true identity, Will. I think it had nothing to do with the cattle war."

"So you think it was just a marvelous coincidence that Jack was also the leader of our group—and a lawyer to boot? Look at what they're doing, Josie. One by one, they're hitting at each of us. They intend to get rid of every last Texan who's challenged 'em."

"Then how do you explain Royce's ambush? He wasn't a Texan, he never openly challenged them—and he was far from a leader in any of this."

"That's true, he wasn't. But they knew he was one of our group, even if most folks *didn't* know that. I think Royce's murder hit two birds with one stone for them."

"You'll have to explain that."

He led me to a place where we could sit. "He was killed the same way as Jack. It happened at the Muddy creek crossing. Someone had sat under the bridge, waited till the wagon had crossed, and shot Royce in the back. To outsiders, it looks like two random acts of violence. But I feel Royce's murder was meant to do two things—get one of us and obscure Weston's motive in killing Jack. Weston, of course, didn't bargain on the eyewitness."

"Has he been charged with both murders?"

"He hadn't been when I left town, but there was strong talk of it. The problem is, there's no evidence linking him to Royce's murder except the similarity. And given that Weston made such a presence of himself in town that morning, the similarity would have proved a slick alibi for him if he hadn't been caught red-handed."

My head was whirling with all this and I felt nauseous. I lay down on the dry grass to give my thoughts a chance to settle and clear.

"I'm sorry to be the bearer of all these bad tidings," he apologized again.

I sighed, wondering. "Do you think Weston acted alone?"

"No. I think he probably planned both murders and accomplished Jack's by himself. But someone else must have killed Royce. Weston was too visible around town to have gotten all the way out to Muddy Creek. The day before the murders, though, he was seen by several people in the company of Gil Herman, and Herman was gone long enough to reach Muddy."

"You think Herman murdered Royce?"

"I do."

"That's a pretty strong accusation, Will."

Gil Herman was the most powerful cattleman in our area. Born in England, he had come to the country as manager for the largest British concern on the northern plains, with three ranches and fifty thousand head of cattle. When the hard winter threw the company into receivership, Herman's years of dedication paid off. On many occasions he had paid the outfit's bills from his own pocket and had consequently become a creditor of no small standing in the court proceeding. In the settlement, he got one of the ranches and ownership of any company cattle found on the range after a Montana man named Wibaux purchased the fifteen thousand head known to have survived the killer winter. Many people marveled at the way Herman kept finding cattle in every nook and coulee after Wibaux went through. In three years, Herman's herd of leftover stock had grown to be the largest in the county.

Gil Herman was by no means the only ranch manager to build a herd at his employer's expense, but he was one of the boldest and cleverest and, along with the Yankton Cattle Company's manager Jimmy Bovin, carried the most power. Bovin had been president of the stock association for years.

Will's accusation was surprising—not because I deemed murder beneath men like Herman or Bovin, but because they paid mercenaries like Weston to do such dirty work for them. The going price for dead Rustlers at that time was $1500 a head, and that was three or four times what most families earned in a year. We weren't supposed to know such things. But Joe Elliot—one of the stock detectives who had hung the horse rancher—bragged one too many times over a bottle and a hand of cards that whenever he got low on funds, he'd just go hang a Rustler and collect another $1500.

Lying there on the cold ground, I wondered angrily if Herman or Weston—both men with families—had ever given consideration to what happens to a victim's family after they've strung the noose or pulled the trigger. Didn't they care about their own wives and children? Didn't they know that their actions could bring retribution in return and visit the same horror on *their* families?

Without speaking a word to him throughout the duration of my life, I vowed that Weston would find no enjoyment in his blood money. He would be made to see the consequences of his actions and live with the knowledge that he had murdered a decent man, widowed a pregnant woman, and deprived four children of their father.

CHAPTER SIX
INJUSTICE AND WRATH
(Excerpt from the Journal of Josie Watson Stewart)

*D*ecember 25, 1891 - *There will never be another Christmas like this. Not if I can help it. For the children's sake I have tried to keep things as normal as possible. But how can I make a normality of Christmas when it follows so closely on the heels of their father's funeral? It only brings the anger in me higher—already a risen tide. I have never been one to espouse hatred of any kind. But I cannot deny this: I hate Ed Weston.*

January 1, 1892 - I have done it. In my anger and gall I have said things I already regret, things which may have irreparably harmed my son and insulted my only friend. Is there no end to the damage this war can cause?

Just thinking of that awful time can still bring back a wrath so strong it causes a palpable bitterness in my mouth. They say one of the best ways to get beyond the painful times of the past is to let the mind relive them and, in doing so, consciously release the anger. Although I have tried these many decades to simply let the dead rest in peace, images have come back to mind, tormenting and uninvited, sudden as a rimrock in my life.

We buried Jack on a small tree-shaded rise in the Willow Grove cemetery near town. Cowboys came from as far away as Miles City and Douglas. If such an occasion can be called beautiful, I guess it was in its fashion. The men were quietly protective of me and the children, hovering about and seeing to our every need. I didn't know more than twenty of them by name, but that didn't stop their silent kindness and heartfelt courtesies. Will clung to my side as inseparably as my own right arm.

The first tide of wrath arose when I went to claim the wagon. The sheriff, kind though he was, insisted apologetically that it was evidence and he must keep it until the court proceedings were over. I requested items from it; after all, it contained our winter supplies, and how else could I expect to feed my family? Even at this, the good sheriff balked. Finally I convinced him it was imperative that I have whatever I could take, and he led me to the shed where it was being held under lock and key. As he opened the doors and the harsh winter sun illuminated the wagon, I understood the sheriff's reluctance.

The sight of it startled me.

"I'm sorry, Mrs. Stewart," said the sheriff. "I didn't want you to see this."

On top of the load in the wagon bed lay the children's Christmas toys, covered in blood as if they also had been murdered.

The sheriff cleared his throat nervously. "He—ah, he fell backward on the load, Mrs. Stewart. That's how we found him. I know this is just awful for you. I can't tell you how sorry I am."

I stared, attempting to maintain composure. "Has Mr. Weston seen this?"

"Please excuse my bluntness, ma'am, but I believe everyone in town has. The wagon—drew quite a crowd when we brought it in. I know it's my job to remain impartial, but given Mr. Charles' testimony, I felt it my moral duty if not my civic one to make certain Mr. Weston saw these toys."

I came back to my senses hearing this. Long before the funeral I had promised myself that my behavior in public would be above reproach. "You're absolutely right, sir," I demurred. "You must remain impartial."

In those days local courts depended on the schedules of the circuit judges, and sessions drew the audience of both town and country dwellers. It was considered a form of education and a diversion from everyday life. Court was in session in December—a fact that would have aided Jack in his attempt to bring Ed Weston swiftly to justice. A hearing was scheduled just days after the funeral. It caused the second tide of anger—one that still has the power to send me into a dark rage.

We expected that the cattlemen would attempt to coerce Mr. Charles into changing his story, which they apparently did. At the hearing he refused to identify the man with the rifle he had seen over Jack's body. As close as he would come was identification of the man's horse, which he stated belonged to his neighbor, Ed Weston. Given that the horse was boarded at a livery in town, where someone could conceivably steal it away for a period of time, this evidence was purely circumstantial and not good enough to prosecute Weston. The presiding judge found insufficient evidence to even hold him on the murder charge.

The sheriff had a series of photographs made of the wagon and released it. We covered the load with a tarp so the children would be spared the sight of the blood, and Will drove us home, fretting under his breath the whole time over what Allison would do when he found out about the hearing. I was in an ugly frame of mind. For once my brother-in-law's fearless impetuosity was a welcome thought.

"He'll do what should have been done months ago," I said, so vehemently Will stared and spoke not another word.

We were both surprised to find Allison cold sober when we got home, and by the look of him Will had had good reason to fret. Even I had to think twice about informing Allison of the hearing, he looked that dangerous. Will convinced me that we had to keep our heads and break the news to Allison in the right way, or the carnage would begin in earnest.

It was Christmas that sent me over the edge. I couldn't get the toys clean. Christmas Eve I scrubbed and scrubbed and still they wore ugly brown stains. Ally was out talking to his horses as Will stood by the table spooning cookie dough onto a bake pan and singing carols in an attempt to brighten my disposition. The children were sleeping.

I stopped my distracted scrubbing as the road to deliverance opened, stark and clear. "Weston doesn't deserve to live," I said.

Will went right on singing as if he hadn't heard.

I landed my fists on the table, sending cookies tumbling, and stared at him. "Do you hear me? I want him dead!"

"You don't mean that, Josie," he said calmly.

"Yes, I do. We'll never put an end to this until we put an end to *him.*"

Suddenly my shawl was in his hands and he was quietly ushering me toward the porch. "Let's take a breath of air," he was saying. "We don't want to wake the children."

The cold night hit with the impudence of a slap in the face. I glared at him, shivering. "A little winter cold isn't going to change my mind. I said I want him dead, and I meant it."

He pulled the shawl's folds up under my chin attentively. "God knows you've earned your wrath, and no one could blame you for talking crazy. But what you need is a good cry, Josie. Do you realize you haven't done that yet? It's all pent up inside and if you don't let it out it'll eat you up like a cancer."

I pushed him away. "I don't need a lecture. I need justice! My children have been deprived of their father forever. I have been deprived of my husband, and you your best friend. It's sheer luck that Weston didn't kill you too! He's a homicidal maniac, and he has to be stopped."

"Josie—"

"Don't you Josie me! I am dead serious!" By now rancor was heating me sufficiently. "You know as well as I that Jack went into town to accomplish the job himself."

Will nodded. "Yes, and I failed him."

"All his friends failed him! You all thought he was just acting crazy!"

"It was my fault, no one else's. I knew him best. I should have seen it. But killing Weston won't bring him back. By god, I hate to see you like this. It can't be good for the baby."

"Well, why don't you try scrubbing toys that are indelibly stained with the blood of your children's murdered father!"

He reached out, but I backed away. "What I want to know, Mr. Standifer, is now that Jack Stewart's gone, who's going to accomplish the job he set out to do?"

We were staring at each other so intently across the silence that neither of us noticed Allison's approach.

"I will," Allison said, and we both jumped at his voice and its determination. He mounted the stair and gazed at Will. "She's right, you know. He enjoys killin'. He's like one of them rogue sheep dogs—once he's had a taste of blood, you'll never break him of killin' sheep."

Will drew in a frustrated breath and turned away, blowing it out in a steam of fog.

"I ain't askin' you to throw in on this with me, Will," Allison said.

Will said nothing, staring pensively at the night.

"Jack was my brother, so I'm the one who *should* do it," Allison added.

Silence.

"Will," I said, "if Allison wants to do it, let him. Somebody has to."

After a time Will turned quietly. "Oddly enough, Jack and I discussed this very thing. After the ambush on me, he came to the same conclusion that you reached tonight, Josie. Neither of us questioned that it needed to be done. But the problem is—as a rule—such a thing doesn't happen legally."

Allison waved a dismissing hand. "I don't care about that."

"I know you don't, Ally," he said. "But Jack did."

"Yeah, and he's dead for tryin' it his way, ain't he, Will?" said Ally. "That's what attemptin' to accomplish things legal gets you in this country. I don't feel obliged to abide by laws that're stacked against us."

"Allison, the last thing your brother wanted was to endanger our cause, and if we were to go off half-cocked and gun Weston down, we'd make a damn martyr of him—pardon me, Josie."

I sighed out a lung full of hot air. I knew he was right. And wasn't it just like Jack to be concerned for Our Glorious Cause above everything—even, ironically, above retribution for his own murder.

Will went on. "I've been thinking about those talks with Jack everyday since he was killed." He looked meaningfully at Allison. "He said the only legal way to do it was in self-defense."

"So let's pick a fight with him," said Allison.

"No, we need to make him pick a fight with one of us. In town, in public view—so there's no question."

"That don't sound too difficult." Allison shrugged.

"He won't rile easy," warned Will.

"We'll find a way to do it."

Will nodded absently. "You know what's the hard part, though? Sure, he's cunning and won't be provoked easy. But—by god, I hate to say this, Josie—he's also an easygoing fella who most folks consider likeable."

"Oh, that makes me sick!" I exclaimed.

"I'm sorry. I know how that sounds, and maybe I didn't come off saying it the way I meant. But it's true. All you know is the stories you've heard about him and what he's done. I ain't saying he's not evil. We all know he is. All I'm saying is, he's good at what he does—he knows how to be *likeable*."

"For heaven's sake, Will!" I erupted. "What do you expect evil to come dressed as—some ugly red thing with horns and a forked tail? *Any*body would have the sense to run from that! It won't come decked out as the Devil. It'll come dressed as an easygoing, likeable man!"

"I know, and I didn't mean to offend you. I chose the wrong words. But it's the truth. And it'll just make it that much harder to get him riled." He tucked the shawl up under my chin again, his eyes on mine like sudden pokes of warning. "He's a family man, you know," he added. "Weston's wife comes from one of the best families in the county. They have two cute little girls."

"Don't." I shook my head.

"I know this ain't what you want to hear, but you have to. Think about whether you can live with this for the rest of your life, because I know you and vengeance don't sit well on your character. Yes, you're mad—with good reason. But don't let one moment of madness ruin you life."

I was close to crying, and I probably should have just let those tears flood my soul right then and there, let them wash me clean and be done with it.

Allison saw me shivering. "Me and Will'll figure everything out. Right now we need to finish those cookies and get Christmas ready for the youngsters."

We didn't speak of it again.

The day after Christmas, the two of them went to town. I didn't ask what they planned to do there. I knew. They had had their heads together most of Christmas day. I didn't try to stop them. It was I, in fact, who set them in motion. If I had never opened my head Christmas Eve, they would never have gone into town.

I didn't stop to think that they were contemplating murder— the very act which had made me a widow and my children fatherless. I didn't take Will's advice and consider that the act's accomplishment would create yet another widow and more fatherless children. I allowed myself to be led only by my rancor and my seemingly righteous vengeance, conveniently thinking of it only as "the deed." I never called it murder in my thoughts. That would have been an admission that I had sunk to Weston's own dark depths.

I should have done all those things.

And I should have cried.

God love Will Standifer. He was the nerviest man I ever met. He had the courage to come back and face me.

That was New Year's Day, 1892.

I still remember the way he sat at the table that evening, looking so defeated he might just lay down and die.

The plan had been to have Allison run into Weston on the street—a simple act of two people passing. But Ally would stop Weston and, offering his hand for the sake of amiable appearances, would say too softly for anyone else to hear: "I'm gonna turn you in, Weston." They expected some nonchalant reply that he would merely return the favor. But Allison would grin and shrug: "Then we'll both go to hell together. But at least when that ol' devil gets me, he won't be getting a back-shooter."

Certainly calling Weston this to his face would provoke a fight. Allison would be unarmed. When Weston touched his gun, Will would come to Ally's defense. If anything could work, this should have been it.

When they got there, the town was abuzz with the news that Mr. Charles had once again grown courageous enough to identify Weston. Another hearing was set for the twenty-eighth. Ally and Will decided to wait and see what transpired in the legal arena.

But as fate would have it, the meeting with Weston on the street happened solely by coincidence. Allison took it as a sign that this was the way it was supposed to go and stopped Weston. Will was ready at his side. Everything went according to plan up through the part of calling Weston a back-shooter. But to their surprise, Weston only grinned and said: "Excuse me, boys. I've got a hearing to attend."

He had sly reason to grin. In spite of Mr. Charles' new testimony, Weston was on his way to freedom. The cattlemen had provided him with a clever attorney who came up with a novel idea of how to get him off.

As Will had said, Gil Herman was suspected as an accomplice in Jack's murder, and this was due to a conversation between Weston and Herman that had been overheard the night before the murder. The conversation made casual mention of Royce Johnson as well, and was all that linked anyone with his murder, albeit circumstantially.

The clever attorney decided that both men should be charged

with both crimes, knowing that if *both* men could not be proved beyond reasonable doubt to be responsible for *both* crimes, *neither could be convicted of either one.*

So when the white cap judge heard both Mr. Charles' new testimony and the evidence of the man who overheard the Herman/Weston conversation, he charged both men with both murders. And then promptly proceeded to release them on thirty thousand dollars bond.

The town was full of rangemen and cowboys, all of whom were following the legal proceedings with restraint. Mass infuriation set in at the perversion of the law and the bonding-out. Herman and Weston, fearing for their lives, left under cover of darkness for Omaha—a place considered a safer haven for cattlemen and stock detectives.

And Will came home to face me with this news.

Allison had had the good sense to stay in town and get annihilatingly drunk.

"I failed you again," Will said, slumping at the table.

I cannot express the depths of my anger at knowing Weston had gotten away yet again. I thought of Jack and how livid he would have been at this clever attorney's flagrant abuse of the law and the judge's complicity. I thought of my children, who would grow up without even the mollification of knowing the legal system had protected their rights by incarcerating the man who had murdered their father. I thought of my future as a widow with four small children to raise.

"Don't worry, Will," I said acidly. "I'm going to raise my son to kill Ed Weston."

How could I have said such a thing?

The statement was no less than a dagger driven into Will's heart. He was already desolate in having failed to accomplish "the deed." The infamous deed. It should have been plain to all of us at that point that we simply were not cut out for nefarious behavior.

But my bitterness filled the room that night. When I made my hideous pronouncement, Will found the strength to stand, nearly in tears, and walk out. I wouldn't see him again for months.

That was bad enough. Worse still, I realized too late that Martin had heard me. I only saw a flicker in the doorway of the children's bedroom, but I knew it was him, awake and listening. I had been too preoccupied since Jack's murder to remember that my son always knew when I was upset and felt it his duty to watch over me. I began to wonder then what manner of damage I had brought on my family with my insidious wrath.

I am telling this now to dispel the myth which seems to have followed me down these long years that I was some sort of saint. I watch this young Mrs. Kennedy, whose husband the President was murdered virtually on her lap in Dallas recently, and I see much of myself in her public demeanor. Perhaps that is why people have thought of me as saintly. While it's true that I made certain my public behavior was nothing short of sterling, I am and freely admit to being most egregiously human.

My saintly public demeanor, beyond having been the proper mode of conduct for a woman in those days, was thoroughly calculated. It was meant to shame Weston and the cattlemen. And if it did, I am not sorry. Shame was the least of what they deserved. But I was no saint, and I have told this part of the story with as much candor as I own to prove that point. As I stated earlier, there were no angels in this affair. War is the tangible definition of insanity. It irrevocably alters every person it touches.

I suppose everyone has a dark side to their soul. I cloistered mine as stealthily as the moon hides her shadowed side. My private little monastery of darkness was at its unholy worst that month after Jack's murder. I suppose it was the concurrent nature of Will's solemn departure and Mart's unfortunate eavesdropping that rattled me enough to steer me back toward the road to daylight and sanity.

CHAPTER SEVEN
INVASION
(Excerpt from the Journal of Josie Watson Stewart)

March 10, 1892 - My third son was born last evening. The delivery was difficult. He is, of course, Jackson Alfred Stewart II. No other name would do. It makes me unbearably sad to realize that Jack will never know this youngest son. I feel so desolate and alone. We have been shut in by a blizzard for nearly three days, winter and its inherent isolation only intensifying the loneliness. I miss Jack so much.

March 15, 1892 - Will visited today. I realized only when I saw him approaching in the snow how much I had missed his presence, and how horrible I must have seemed in December. But even after an abject apology for my insane behavior, he seemed distant and sad, preoccupied. Try though I might, I couldn't quite reach him. I hope he is not concealing an illness.

It's a miracle I didn't bleed to death bringing young Jack into the world. I knew early on that something was amiss and had Martin fetch Mrs. Burgee. She was a quiet woman, and I think a bit afraid of me. Timidity aside, she managed to stop the hemorrhage before I was lost to this world. The exhaustion and loss of blood only made my winter depression deeper. Mrs. Burgee stayed at my bedside for two whole days, forsaking her own family and managing mine instead. Mart took over after that, until I could get up and around.

The first day I was ambulatory Will showed up. It did my heart a world of good to see him, though I must have looked a sight.

I wasn't out of my nightclothes yet, for I couldn't be on my feet more than a half hour at a time. I don't think I had brushed my hair in a week. I was rocking young Jack by the stove when he came in. He drew a chair next to us.

"I heard you had another boy," he smiled. "I'd lay a bet on what you named him."

"I'm so glad to see you, Will."

"That makes two of us. Are you feeling alright? You're looking pale."

"We had a hard time."

"I'm sorry I wasn't closer."

"I'm sorry I ran you off in January."

He shook his head. "You didn't."

"Yes, I did. I was crazy, and I apologize. I had no right to drag you into my insanity and try to make you do those horrid things."

"You don't need to apologize."

"Yes, I do. And I need to apologize to Allison, too, but I haven't seen him since Christmas."

Will looked alarmed. "He hasn't been around?"

"Oh, he's been around, but I never see him. He comes in the night to make sure the chores are done, then vanishes before daylight. I know he thinks I hate him worse than ever, but I don't. I don't hate him at all. In a strange way, I understand him better now."

"Ally's a good-hearted person, Josie. He'll never have Jack's polish and shine, but there's not a more loyal or fearless soul in this world."

"I know. I've been harder on him than he deserved."

"He's never faulted you for that."

"He wouldn't. It's not in his nature. But that doesn't excuse it. Do you ever see him?"

He shook his head. "He must be hiding."

"I just hope he's not drinking."

"I'll gamble he is. He was kicking himself mighty hard about the way that Weston thing came out."

I sighed. "That was my fault."

"Naw—Allison was set on trying something before you ever opened your head, Josie. The only difference is, now he thinks your hopes were riding on it and it amounts to one more way he's been a disappointment. He may be a fearless man, but he's scared to death of you."

"Maybe I should leave him a note in the stable and tell him I'm sorry. I don't want him to live his life like this."

"Ally'll be alright. But a note probably wouldn't hurt." He leaned forward and peeked at the baby. "He's a good-lookin' little crittur, ain't he."

"You want to hold him?"

"Sure, I'll give him a try."

I rose. "You two get acquainted. I need to brush my hair."

I was surprised at the ease with which he handled the baby. Isn't that funny? If it had been a girl, he probably would have been so nervous he would have fallen off that chair trying not to break her. I remember how intimidated he was by Alexanne when she was a baby, and there he sat talking to young Jack like they were lifelong friends. It's hard to figure men sometimes.

He had talked the baby nearly to sleep by the time I returned. It was nice to have a few minutes to do something for myself. Will didn't seem in a hurry to give young Jack up, so I took my time, knowing such moments would be few and far between in my future. I put up some coffee for us. When Martin took the other children out to feed the horses, Will looked at me with a pensive seriousness.

"Will you ever marry again, Josie?"

"No," I declared, though it wasn't exactly true. I probably would have married him if he had ever asked. We had such a solid friendship, and there's nothing on earth that can make for a better marriage than that. On the other hand, maybe he *was* asking me at that moment and I was just too dumb to realize it. In retrospect, I recall his look took on a hint of wounded pride when I delivered my determined answer. But I misread it at the time. I just thought he wasn't feeling well.

"I want you to know," he said, "that me and the boys'll take care of your range stock. And I'll be here to do whatever I can for you whenever you need anything. I'll come by and check on you as often as possible."

"Thank you, Will. I appreciate that."

"I should've come sooner."

"After the way I ran you off New Year's Day, I consider it a miracle that you came back at all."

"It wasn't that," he said. "You didn't run me off. It's just—I got to thinking that maybe it didn't look right, me being here so much. You know, with Jack gone. People might get to talkin'."

"Will, we have too close a friendship to worry about such things."

"I would never want to do anything that might hurt you and the kids."

I reached out and touched his shoulder. "It would hurt us all unbearably if you stayed away. You know the children wouldn't understand it. You're all we have, so please don't do that."

"I'll come as often as I can," he said, but there was some vague finality in his voice that I couldn't interpret.

Maybe he sensed what April would bring. Maybe he loved me beyond our friendship and was dispirited because I could not see it.

Maybe he was just having a rough day.

Things changed in our little valley that spring. John Burgee decided that the best way to champion our cause to the world was by becoming editor of a newspaper. One of the papers in town was for sale, and he managed to put together enough cash to buy it. Whit Fielder, who had recently married, bought out Burgee's share of their ranch and became our neighbor.

There has always been a special place in my heart for Whit. He was the best neighbor I ever had. But he was more than that. We grew into a friendship, over the years, as solid as the one with Will. I know it was largely due to the fact that these men were Jack's closest boyhood pals and felt it their duty to watch over us, but I couldn't have hand-picked a finer set of friends.

Jack would have been proud of them.

Many years later Whit would tell me that gaining him for a neighbor was all part of their plan. At the time, it just seemed wonderfully convenient that Burgee—who was always somewhat aloof—had had the urge to become a newspaperman just when Whit married and was ready to start raising a family. But once in the early 1920s Whit and I were thinking back on Will's life and he told me that right after young Jack was born Will came to him.

"He musta knowed what was comin', Josie," Whit said, "because he convinced me that I needed to move my bride into the ranch house where we could keep an eye on you. 'Course I said John Burgee might have something to say about that, since he was livin' there. But Will said, 'Let's buy him out, Whit—I'll help you. He's been wanting to take over that paper anyhow. Josie needs one of us close by, and you got a better chance of living longer than I do.' Course it always worried me when Will'd talk like that, cuz ever since he was a kid I felt he was a little clairvoyant."

I must admit, it eased my mind to know Whit was my neighbor. I still hadn't seen Allison, although I had left a note in the stable with his name on it. That note sat there for weeks and he never touched it. I finally removed it when I realized it was pitch dark when he came to do the chores and he would probably never find it. Not long after Whit moved in, Allison stopped coming around so regularly. I heard he was drunk a good deal of the time, and that made me sad. By then I was able to resume most of the chores anyhow. Whit took over with the heavy stuff.

His bride Gussie wasn't the brightest woman in the world, but she was lighthearted and amiable and I got on with her fine. She was quite good-looking, too, which was a pleasure to all the cowboys. They sure appreciated a pretty face, especially when it came decked out with a smile like Gussie's. Whit and Gussie had just finished moving in the day of the invasion. Burgee was taking out the last of his things.

There is no easy way to tell the story of how the cattlemen invaded our country, so I'll say it as bluntly as it happened. In the early morning hours of April 9, some fifty-odd heavily-armed men surrounded the place Will Standifer was leasing on the plains and commenced shelling the cabin. He held them off for better than ten hours single-handedly.

All that spring, unbeknownst to us, the cattlemen had had an emissary down in Texas recruiting mercenaries for the job of ridding "their range" of a pack of thieves. Put that way, any man would assume we were worth the effort of extermination. Twenty-some men had been recruited by April and joined again as many cattlemen and stock detectives for the excursion. There was over a hundred thousand dollars in the market seizure fund, which the cattlemen used to finance their excursion. How's that for a rude paradox—they used the money acquired from stealing and selling *our* stock to wage armed warfare on us.

The invaders were provided with brand new Winchesters, two hundred rounds of ammunition apiece, five dollars per diem, a list of names, and a promise of a fifty dollar bonus for every dead Rustler. A special train left Cheyenne, bringing them with their horses as far north as the railway went at that time, then they traveled under cover of darkness into our country, cutting the telegraph wires to insure that we couldn't call for help.

I know it sounds like I'm manufacturing purple prose again, but I couldn't make up something this atrocious.

Whit came up my steps with Gussie in tow the morning of April 10. "Gussie, see to the kids. I need to talk to Josie," he said.

He took me to the porch. I had never seen such a brusque manner on Whit. But once we stood there alone, he took my hands gently in his.

"Will's been killed," he said.

"No! Don't say these things, Whit, I can't stand it!"

"Get a hold of yourself, now. I'm tellin' you Will's dead. And there's an armed body of assassins loose in the country."

That dropped me straight down to earth. *"What?"*

"They killed him."

"Assassins. You mean stock detectives?"

"Them and cattlemen and a bunch of hired guns. They killed Will and were about to do the same to every one of us men who've bucked their authority, but Will held 'em off long enough for someone to get the sheriff and a posse. Burgee was one of the first to discover them. They fired on him and his stepson, but the two of 'em got away. I'm told we got the whole bunch of the murderin' SOBs surrounded at the TA ranch a few miles south of town."

"We? Who do you mean?"

Whit smiled. "There's some three hundred cowboys, farmers, and rangemen that've got 'em holed up and ready to give 'em hell— pardon me."

"What about the sheriff and posse?"

"We *are* the posse," Whit grinned. "The sheriff's gone to see if he can get the assistance of the cavalry to bring 'em to justice. I just came over to give you the news and deposit Gussie with you. You two stick together till I get back, keep the windows covered at night, and have your firearms handy. You shouldn't have any trouble, but be ready for it anyhow. And stay in the house. Don't worry about the chores. Allison's up on the hill there. He'll see to the animals and make sure nobody comes into the valley uninvited. I'm gonna go help our boys lay siege."

A chalky lump formed in my throat. "Whit, are you sure about Will?"

He squeezed my hand. "He made a mighty brave stand-off, Josie. Held fifty men off all day. Now, if you'll excuse me, I'm gonna go take a shot or two at the bastards who kilt him."

Suddenly the tears came. The dam broke and they finally came pouring out of me in a silent torrent. I cried for both of them, Jack and Will. And for me—a lonely widow. I cried for my children, who would never know their father, or his best friend—and for all the sad casualties in that God-forsaken war.

Gussie came out and kissed Whit good-bye, then put an arm around my shoulders as I stood there, tears streaming uncontrolled down my face. To her credit she said nothing, just braced me there for a few minutes, then went back to watch over the children.

Ever the knowing one, Mart came out to soothe me without even the knowledge of what made me cry. He just rubbed my back and let the deluge happen. Like Will, he seemed to know how desperately I needed to grieve.

I won't go into great detail about the invasion and its aftermath, primarily because it's already in the history books, and because it still breaks my heart to talk about it. Losing Will really took the wind out of me. It was as if the cattlemen had poured an ocean of salt on my wounded soul. It didn't help to know that Gil Herman and Ed Weston were counted among the invaders. But it didn't surprise me.

The group had grandiose plans of killing every blackballed rancher in our country, and even blowing up the courthouse in town to get rid of the outstanding warrants against Weston and Herman. What they managed to do was kill Will and a friend who was recuperating from a horse accident at his place before three hundred angry citizens rose up against them. The sheriff tried to telegraph for the National Guard but found the wires mysteriously down. So he deputized a citizen posse.

While the citizens had the invaders cornered at the TA ranch, the sheriff went to Fort McKinney and attempted to get the assistance of the cavalry. They said they couldn't act without orders from their division commander in Omaha. And of course the wires were down, so communication with Omaha was out of the question. On April 12, the wires were up long enough for the sheriff to contact the governor requesting assistance of the National Guard in suppressing an insurrection.

The governor had already heard by special courier that his cattle cronies were surrounded in enemy territory. Rather than give the good sheriff the requested assistance, he sent an urgent wire to President Harrison in Washington, who in turn granted him the resources of the entire War Department. The cavalry came immediately to the cattlemen's rescue.

They were whisked away to the capital, where, the governor contended, they were safer. For the five months of their incarceration—which amounted to a lax case of house arrest—they were boarded at the expense of our tax dollars, which bled the county dry of the funds with which to prosecute them. In August, they were released. The Texas mercenaries went home fully paid.

As in the cases of the unfortunate couple lynched in 1889, the horse rancher dry-gulched in June of 1891, and the back-shooting murders of Jackson A. Stewart and Royce Johnson, no one was ever tried or convicted of the murders of Will Standifer and his recuperating friend. Through the abuse of money and power, the cattlemen had perfected their self-law-proofing act by then.

Even when they lost, they won.

CHAPTER EIGHT
AFTERMATH
(Excerpt from the Journal of Josie Watson Stewart)

December 1, 1892 - I have survived a year without Jack. Some days it seems infinitely longer. I doubt I will ever get over losing him. How does one overcome tragedy when it is an ongoing affair? I have tried to distance myself from this war ever since the Invasion, tried to establish among the wreckage some measure of normality in my children's lives. But the rancor and violence make a constant annoying presence of themselves, altering the personalities of the most staid citizens. People live in a persistent state of agitation, fear having given way to anger, and the smallest infraction of protocol can easily be construed as provocation. Without Jack's level-headed legal opinion and Will's firm example, a darker side of our men's characters has emerged. At every opportunity I have counseled against revenge and violence, even where it applies to language and idle threats, but I am one minuscule voice in an angry roar demanding justice. And justice is not forthcoming. What hurts the most is seeing our men descend into behavior which all but mirrors that of the cattlemen. We are becoming that which we most despise. How does one stop such a thing from happening in a war? It might be easier to reverse a landslide.

April 9, 1893 - Another dubious achievement: I have now lived a whole year without Will. I still think of him every time I step onto the porch—it seems so much of our friendship was spent there. And I miss him nearly as much as Jack. I envision them together in a place where there is no war and no such thing as missing, a place where peace and justice reign supreme. And I envy them.

One might imagine that the atmosphere on the range after the Invasion was none too pleasant. I must say, though, if ever that country belonged to us, that was our time of ownership. The cattlemen and their sympathizers were smart enough to make themselves as scarce as possible for the next several months. When encounters were inevitable, the white caps were like obedient children all of a sudden—seen but not heard. And our cowboys, being by and large a vociferous bunch when provoked, perpetrated on them and their affiliates a great deal of verbal abuse. Not only did our men berate all white caps during conversations among themselves, they were incensed enough to berate them to their faces. Tyranny was a thing that might be rebelled against by a handful of nervy men on the range. Murder, arson and invasion were quite another issue altogether. No one could sit quietly in the face of such crimes. The cattlemen's demonstration of their infinite ability to evade prosecution only added fuel to our men's fire.

Even though I knew the wrath was perfectly justifiable, I remembered what it had done to me the winter of Jack's death and knew what a fine line anyone walks who gives in to it. I tried at every opportunity to dissuade our men from embracing violence, but I was wasting my breath. The tension had been building for too long—release was inevitable.

"Look at it this way," Whit tried to explain, "our boys ain't shootin' anybody in the back, they're just abusin' 'em with words. It's the least of what the SOBs deserve for what they done."

"I understand that, Whit. But where does it end? Doesn't someone have to make the first move toward peace? Our children have to grow up here. Do you realize what they're learning?"

"We all admire your intentions, Josie. After what you been through, by the gods, you're a saint. But a little verbal abuse is quite likely the only form of justice these snakes'll ever see. So leave the boys to their task. It needs doing."

So I left them to their task, and distanced myself from the world as best I could. I had a ranch to run and children to raise. I let Nature be my adversary.

She was less predictable than the cattlemen, but on the whole kinder and without pretense. And even though she was prone to seasonal fits of wrath, she was neither arrogant nor imperious. When she chose violence she spread it indiscriminately among us all—rich and poor, humans and animals, cattlemen and settlers alike. To her, we were indistinguishable from the land. I appreciated that. I was in a frame of mind that made me more agreeable to being allied with the land than with my fellow man. I liked to think that she favored me just a little. My valley was protected from most of her inclemencies. Winters, though snowy, were never so harsh as they were on the plains. Summers were cooler, and the wind was never the demon to us it was to plains dwellers. But it never pays to underestimate Mother Nature. About the time I began to think I was in her favor, she set me straight.

The winter of 1892-3 didn't seem significantly snowier than previous winters, so I could not have foreseen the flood. Whit said it was the sudden warm spell in April that melted the snow-pack in the mountains above us quicker than usual. Our innocuous little waterway rose like a tidal wave, covering the hay-meadows and sending the horses to the side-hills in befuddlement. The valley became a lake, our house an island in its midst. The children were fascinated and caught fish bare-handed from the porch. The diversion was less than entertaining for me. I worried that the water would rise higher and ruin more household goods—or worse, wash us away. I worried that the hay would be ruined for the year, and that the children would get carried away with their fish catching and drown.

I learned a keener respect for Nature that spring.

As the water began receding, a fresh worry surfaced: snakes. They were everywhere and clung to anything resembling dry land, which our house became for them. For the most part they were harmless garters and bull snakes, but we had some rattlers too, much to my chagrin. I know it's simply a manifestation of my Christian upbringing, but I detest snakes. Not even omnipotent Mother Nature could make me appreciate them.

Mart and Henry manned a pitchfork apiece and stayed on snake detail for five days running. It gave them a manly pride to show off their snake talents to their sister and baby brother, although Alexanne came out of the affair looking more like their supervisor than someone they were sworn to protect. "Over here, boys!" I would hear her shout every time she located another slithering intruder. Whit came by several times during the flood, swimming his horse right up to the porch.

With natural disasters to contend with, I had little time to worry about the latest insult in the cattle war. And, frankly, I was glad to put it out of my head. At least with Mother Nature there was calm before and after the storms. With the cattlemen, it was one long drawn-out inclement affair, oppressive and cynical, spiked by outbreaks of lethal violence.

When George Melvin was killed by ambush, I resigned myself to a mental vow of silence and refused to engage in conversations about the cattle war. Melvin was the boss who threw Jed Argand out of round-up for illegally attempting to brand suckling calves.

Right after the Invasion, Melvin had accepted a position of Deputy United States Marshal. He had long been foreman for one of the big outfits, was a loyal company man, but in spite of his affiliations with the cattlemen was well liked among our men for his honesty and competence as a rangeman. In fact they rejoiced that someone as respectable as George was accepting a federal law position, feeling that he was a man who might judge both sides fairly.

The cattlemen tried every way they could to pin his murder on us, even tried to coerce the President into instituting martial law to "control" us. When the President pointed out that conditions were legally insufficient for a declaration of martial law, they devised a clever plot which they felt certain would end the cattle war in their favor. There was a lot of finger-pointing and name-calling on both sides when Melvin was killed. Jimmy Bovin, manager of the Yankton Cattle Company and Invader First Class, wrote a letter to his friends, our cattlemen Senators in Washington, outlining a strategy he was sure would end things suitably:

Since—he surmised—most of the troublemakers were Texas cowboys and Southern Democrats with Rebel sympathies, if the governor were to call in the colored troops to maintain order, it would so infuriate the cowboys that violence would erupt and the President would have reason to declare martial law. Whereupon the War Department could send in more cavalry and eradicate the troublemakers. This would neatly accomplish what the cattlemen had originally set out to do.

I wouldn't have believed it possible, but I have a copy of Bovin's letter to prove that he hatched the scheme to bring in the 9th and 10th cavalries.

Bovin was certain our Texans would rebel in high order at being baby-sat by the colored troops. But the only mishap that occurred while they were in our country was a fight that erupted between two troopers over a card game.

Many of our men felt certain the cattlemen themselves had had Melvin killed simply to create another excuse to continue their campaign of extermination. This may have seemed logical to me once, but by then I had given up engaging in speculations of the cattle war. I simply left the room or stepped outside when the subject came up. I spent a lot of time by myself those days, even at social gatherings, because there didn't seem to be any other topic of conversation worth discussing to most folks.

The preponderance of evidence pointed to Jed Argand as Melvin's killer. He was witnessed in Melvin's presence just moments before the ambush, and even though Melvin's pearl-handled pistol was never found, someone testified to having seen it in Argand's possession, which gave the grand jury enough evidence for an indictment. By that time, Argand had skipped the country.

The cattlemen tried their best to prove Argand was one of us, but fell short. Argand was a known thief and suspected murderer. Nobody wanted to sit next to that kind of reputation. Besides, our men were madder at Melvin's murder than the cattlemen ever bargained on, and that sort of spontaneous reaction is hard to discredit. Less than two years later word came into our country that Argand had been killed in a gunfight somewhere in Canada.

But it was Billy Shaw who finally settled the issue of Argand's guilt in 1936. He was an old man then and had been living in California for many years. He came to visit us that spring, and we went for a drive in his automobile so he could see his old stomping grounds one last time. Billy was a wiry, good-natured man and had a story for every creek and draw we traversed. It was just the three of us—Billy, Mart, and me. I was no spring chicken myself then—Mart was almost fifty and had been county sheriff for many years.

We drove all over the countryside, many of the cow trails having become passable dirt roads by then. Presently Billy pulled to a stop, looking up at a rock outcrop that stood off to our right several hundred yards.

"Let's take a walk," he said, and we all got out of the vehicle. It was a blustery day, cold for that late in May.

He took his time, holding my elbow as we talked and climbed up toward the rock outcrop. It was quite steep near the top. I assumed the purpose was to sit and enjoy the view, which we did. After a few minutes, though, Billy started rummaging around in the rocks. There was an overhang there, not quite a cave, and he was tossing over every rock in there. Finally he stopped, sat back on his heels a moment, then wrestled a rusty old five-pound baking soda can from beneath the rocks.

"I'll be damned," he said, which surprised me because Billy wasn't prone to profanity, especially in the presence of women. He handed the can to Mart.

"What's this?" Mart inquired.

"I'll bet you a hundred dollars it's George Melvin's pistol," said Billy. "But I hope I'm wrong."

"George Melvin's?" Mart looked amazed.

"Uh-huh. You remember who he was?"

"Sure, I do. They never found his pistol, as I recall."

Billy was nodding, staring off across the plains. "I was gatherin' stock in this country that October, camped just over yonder on the river past where that sheep herder's wagon is. And one night, who should come into camp but Jed Argand and a coupla his shady pals.

They was purty drunked up and talkin' mighty tall, and Argand brags on killin' a lawman. 'Course I'd been out range ridin' for several weeks and hadn't heard about Melvin. I waddn't much impressed with Argand's talk and he could see I waddn't, so he told me, 'Go up to that overhang, if you don't believe me. I buried his pistol in a soda can up there—damn nice piece, too,' he says—beg yer pardon there, Josie. Then he sized me up and told me I could look at it, but if he come back and it was gone he'd hunt me down and kill me too. 'Course I waddn't no more scared of Jed Argand that I was a bedbug. I jest thought he was a-braggin'. He was knowed for bein' quite a loud-mouthed some'buck."

"And you never told anyone?" asked Mart.

"No, and I never looked for that soda can neither. Not till today."

"How come?" Mart wondered.

"I didn't want nothin' to do with it. By the time I heard about Melvin it was too late anyhow. Argand had already slipped the country. Ever'body purty much knowed it was him who kilt George, and I didn't want no part of it."

"But, Billy, you might've provided the evidence needed to convict Argand," Mart said.

He was a good sheriff, if I do say so myself.

Billy looked at him. "You was purty young then, Mart. Do you recollect at all what it was like around here durin' the cattle war?"

"Yes, I remember it quite clear."

"Then you may recall that if I jest happened to find George Melvin's gun, they'd've suspicioned me jest as much as they did Argand. It was evidenced that there was two more unidentified men in on Melvin's ambush, and the cattlemen would've liked nothin' better than to link my name with Argand's in the indictment. I was on their list, you know."

Mart conceded. "I expect you're right."

"Besides," Billy added, "Melvin was too well-liked among our crowd. I knowed him personally, and I didn't want nothin' to do with Argand or his shady dealin's."

"I understand," said Mart.

"So, let's settle this thing. Open 'er up, Mart."

Inside the can was a piece of burlap and a bunch of dirt, nothing more.

Billy issued a sigh of relief and shook his head. "I been worryin' over this for more'n forty years. I shoulda knowed Argand was jest a loudmouthed so-and-so. I still say he kilt Melvin, though."

Mart cleared his throat. "Well, there's no doubt the man was a braggart, Billy. But I don't think he was talkin' through his hat, exactly. You say you knowed Melvin. Did you ever see his gun?"

"Oh, yes. He showed it to me jest after he got it. It was a brand new double-action .45 Colt's. I never knowed anyone else to carry a pistol quite like it. It had been a gift from the man he worked for, you see, and it was the fanciest piece I ever laid eyes on. Nickel-plated, and it had them mother-of-pearl inlays. The handle was rounded on the bottom, so it fit in yore hand jest perfect."

"I believe I've seen that very gun," Mart said.

"Where?" Billy looked at him.

"See that old fella standing away over yonder?"

"The sheep herder?"

"Uh-huh. Name's Alex White," said Mart. "He come to me about five years ago with a gun. Said he found it in an old five-pound soda can under an outcrop above the river where he herds his sheep. Since it was such a fancy piece he figured he better bring it to me. He didn't wanna have to answer any questions as to where a poor sheepherder got such a pistol. So I put it in safekeeping and looked back through twenty-five years worth of files to see if such a piece had been reported stolen or missing. I couldn't find anything. 'Course, it never occurred that it might be Melvin's. His murder was ancient history by then. After holding it for two, three years without claim, I reckoned it belonged to the man who found it. So I give it back to Alex. I'll gamble it's sittin' over in his sheep wagon right now."

"You don't say." Billy shook his head.

"I expect he'd let us have a look at it, if you think you could identify it as Melvin's," Mart said.

"I reckon I could."

So we climbed down and went to Alex White's camp. Mart explained that he had someone who might identify the owner of the gun, if Alex still had it.

"Oh, sure!" he said, and disappeared into his wagon. When he brought it out, Billy scrutinized it, turning it over in his hands.

"If that ain't George Melvin's gun, it's one jest exactly like it," he said.

Alex White stood back, shocked. "George Melvin?—you mean that young lawman who was kilt away back in the days of the cattle war?"

"Uh-huh," Mart nodded. "You remember that?"

"Why, yes sir! And if it's all the same to you, Mart, I'd rather not have that gun."

"Well, Alex, I was just thinkin' maybe you'd like to donate it to the museum in town."

"You take it, Mart. Wouldn't do for an old sheep herder to be carryin' such a piece, anyhow. Do what you want with it."

When the old-time cowboys heard George Melvin's pistol was in the museum, they came to inspect it. All who had known him agreed it had to be Melvin's gun. Nobody else in our country ever had one like it.

I told of the oral drumming our boys gave the cattlemen after the invasion, and I should mention that it was enough of an intimidation that many white caps wouldn't go anywhere in the county without a bodyguard. Those cattlemen who had actually taken part in the invasion felt the need for even greater protection and retained a flank of their most trusted hands or stayed out of the country entirely. Gil Herman was a notable exception.

To everyone's surprise, upon release from incarceration—unlike Weston—Herman actually came back to the county. He eventually brought his family home from the sanctity of Denver as well, and proceeded to go on with his life. He even offered himself to the court on the Stewart-Johnson double murder charges. People have called that a courageous move, but Herman knew they had no evidence that could convict him, and I believe he wanted to extricate himself from the mess and distance himself from Weston. Herman's friend, the judge, reviewed the case and dropped all charges against him—but not Weston.

Gil Herman was a small, delicate-looking man who, with his English accent and close-clipped beard, had the visage more of a literary scholar than a cowman. Though most of our men hated him vehemently for what he had done, they couldn't help but admire his nerve in coming back and going about unguarded. It opened him up to more numerous confrontations of ridicule than his more protected cronies suffered, but he seemed to take it in stride. Though never obsequious or apologetic, he faced the insults, made no word in reply, and went about his business when the hazing was finished.

As much as I would like to believe verbal abuse was the extent of our compensatory activities, I must be candid and tell the whole story. I will admit to taking a risk, for it is the opinion of our side—and with good reason—that much of what happened has been taken out of context by the cattlemen and used to justify their actions. Because of this, most of our people have been skeptical of telling anything, let alone everything. So I proceed on the belief that you will be fair in assessing the situation *in its entirety.*

For more than a decade prior to the invasion the cattlemen had decried settlers as beefers, and during all that time the instances where it was true were so few as to engender a proper outrage at such a blatant prejudice. In the aftermath of the invasion a great many settlers and cowboys who had never beefed a steer in their lives gave in to anger and started killing stock, and not just for beef either. One couldn't travel any road or trail in our country without seeing dead steers galore—mostly Yankton and Herman stuff—left to rot in the sun, strewn over the plains as if by a killing wind.

I knew the boys felt perfectly justified in their actions as retribution for the tyranny, murder, and terror, and for the message it sent to the cattlemen. The act was symbolic, of course. It wasn't an act of killing cattle, it was an act of bringing the cattlemen's worst fears to life, an ominous fulfillment of the "enormous depredations" paranoia that had haunted the cattlemen for years—an actuation of their unreasoning fear of losing their profits. Cattle had always been worth more than good men to the white caps. The killing of beef was meant to get their attention in the only language they understood—the rhetoric of financial statements—and show them the error of their greed. No one begrudges an honest businessman his profit—that's what business is all about. But murder, arson, and terror are crimes against humanity, and to do such things for the sake of profit makes the crimes all the more insidious. Thieves, were we? Our boys made certain the cattlemen understood one thing: *No one would profit from dead, rotting steers.*

I am certain our men felt this was justification enough for the slaughter, but further absolution could be achieved from the fact that at least they were not taking *human* lives. But it was still a wasteful taking of life, as far as I was concerned, and only served to play directly into the cattlemen's hand. They had called us beefers for years. We had somehow lived up to the name.

I don't know how many times I heard Whit say: "This goes way beyond the concept of beefin', Josie. None of these little fellas ever went to killin' beef till the white caps went to killin' men." I suppose, in his mind, it was more or less a hoof-for-an-eye philosophy. The statement was usually followed with: "We never killed a man, and by the gods we *never* shot anybody in the back."

Maybe our differences on the issue derive from somewhere in the disparity between male and female views on life in general. Perhaps women, who give life, are less likely than men to condone the taking of life. I guess I should feel somewhat appeased that our men modified the biblical edict into a *hoof* for an eye. Perhaps that shows some measure of evolutionary progress. Maybe in another millennium or two we will have progressed beyond violence altogether.

But I believe mankind must address the issue of greed first.

CHAPTER NINE
LIFE ON THE PLAINS
(Excerpt form the Journal of Josie Waston Stewart)

*J*uly 4, 1893 - *Whatever in the world shall I do with Allison? That man simply cannot seem to behave in a normal fashion, no matter what. It's bad enough that we are nearly destitute for lack of being able to market our beef and the absence of a hay crop to sell this year. I have used up nearly all of the money left me from my mother's estate just keeping my family alive. These are enough worries without adding Allison's inevitable indiscretions to the stew. Sometimes I wish I could just sprout wings and fly away from all of this.*

August 28, 1893 - In an odd way, I guess my wish has been granted. Tomorrow morning we leave for the plains. I hope things will go smoother for us there. It's only a temporary move, but I will miss my little valley and the comfort of its red walls embracing me, the vista of its long meadows. I do not look forward to the barren reaches of grass, nor the heat and wind of the open plains. But this cannot be avoided. We need the money. And even though teaching school will not make me rich, at least I will have an income for the next year. Whit has promised to look after things for us. I know he will do a good job of it.

Back in those days people went to greater lengths to put on a Fourth of July affair than they do anymore. Oh, the parties now have fancier trimmings, but the community doesn't seem to get involved in the way we used to, and we were scattered over miles of open country. We didn't have many resources, but we somehow managed to put together enough food for a feast, and somebody always came up with enough beer—which could have been left out as far as I saw it. We would gather at a predetermined spot and have quite a crowd for three or four days. People who had tents or teepees would bring them; some folks would sleep under their wagons and some would sleep in the open. That July of '93 someone brought an old circus tent big enough for several families.

Sometime in the middle of the first night a bad wind came up and liked to have blown that tent into the next county. Men were holding poles up and the edges down, but they were losing the battle. Gussie Fielder thought it would be helpful to light a lamp so the men might see what they were up against. She never could figure out why five women tackled her as if she committed a perversity. Like I say, Gussie wasn't the brightest woman in the world. Besides the fact that a lighted lamp was a safety hazard in a high wind, it never dawned on her that three quarters of the adults in that tent had no clothes on.

That was also the time when my feud with Allison rekindled with a vengeance. And we had been doing so well.

After Jack was ambushed, Allison was an unholy mess. I had never seen him drunker and more disheveled—when I saw him at all. He hid out in the hills above the homestead and came down to the stable to do the chores during the night. When the chores would go undone for days in a row, I knew he had gone to town for more liquor. After Will was murdered, Allison's trips to town grew more frequent and lengthy.

It was autumn of '92 that he finally began to snap out of it. He had developed a disturbing cough and Whit managed to convince him another winter outdoors would be his undoing. Although I do not believe the possibility of death bothered Allison one iota, I do believe the thought occurred that he was shirking a familial duty to his dead brother's children. Perhaps it dawned on him that he needed to teach Mart and Henry how to handle cattle and run a ranch before he drank himself into the final oblivion. For nearly nine months he was sober as a judge.

And he was actually pleasant to have around. He seemed to have outgrown his fear of me and settled into what I could only describe as a deferential kindness in my presence. He spent a good deal of time with Mart, taking him out to the range for a multitude of cow lessons, teaching him foremost how to handle a rope and the art of cutting calves for branding. And this truly was an art.

It never ceases to amaze me that when cattle herds are shown in movies, inevitably cowboys are chasing them, swinging big loops and raising a noisy ruckus. I never saw such a thing in real life, short of a stampede. Running cattle can make them lose ten pounds in thirty minutes—not an attractive prospect when market weight is supposed to be your livelihood. Any cowboy who stirred up a herd in attempting to rope a calf wasn't much of a hand. Of course, the real thing wouldn't have been very exciting for a movie audience. The smoother the cowboy was at cutting, the less action there was. Allison was naturally good at this because of his knack with horses, but Billy Shaw was the best. Whit used to say, "Billy was the smoothest I ever saw. If he was workin' a herd, they'd all be lyin' down."

I must say, when Allison made up his mind to do something he went after the whole hog. He gave every daylight hour to Mart's ranching education. He had included Henry in the beginning, but it became apparent right away that Henry had no inclination toward the cowboy life. He preferred to help around the house and if given a free moment would gladly put his nose in a book. It was obvious that Mart would run the ranch—although if Alexanne had had her druthers, she would have given him a fair run for the title of foreman.

"Girls cain't be foremen," Mart informed her.

"Why not?" she challenged.

"Cuz they're girls, not men. Foremen are men."

"You ain't no man, Mart Stewart. Heck, you ain't even seven years old."

"Don't matter. Girls cain't run ranches."

"Oh, yes they can! Mama does."

"That's different. She wouldn't if she didn't have to. Now, quit your fussin' and help me feed the horses."

"You're the foreman, do it yourself. Girls cain't run ranches, 'member?"

"That don't mean they cain't help run 'em."

"I ain't movin' a hair till you take it back. I'd be a good foreman, and you know it, Smarty Pants."

"It's just a simple fact, Lex. Girls ain't cut out for runnin' ranches."

"Mama seems to do it just fine."

"That's only cuz Daddy died."

"Well, who's gonna run the ranch if *you* die, Mr. Know-it-All? Betcha it won't be Henry."

She certainly had him there.

"Alright," he conceded, "I guess you can start as wrangler. Now, quit arguin' and take care of them horses."

Allison overheard this conversation and immediately began including Alexanne in all the outside chores. He never took her to the range, but he taught her to use a rope and imparted to her his wealth of horse savvy. She was a wrangler, alright. And she wore the title well. I think there must have been something about her that reminded Allison of his little sister, Leigh. He clearly enjoyed being around Alexanne. And he allotted time each evening for Henry and the baby, usually entertaining Young Jack while Henry read them all a story.

But his love for Mart was especially deep.

The three ranch hands in the family—Ally, Mart, and Alexanne—had become inseparable by spring. Allison was a good teacher. His patience with those youngsters was astounding. To see him that way was both a joy and a sorrow. The joy was in seeing him sober and doing something at which he was uniquely talented. The sorrow came from knowing it probably would not endure, that he would eventually disintegrate. I was never able to understand how a man with his abilities could waste his life so recklessly. It was a rotten shame.

In his mind, I suppose Allison thought he was just continuing their cowboy education at the Fourth of July party. Perhaps it was my fault for not watching over them more closely in that crowd, but I had grown so accustomed to having them in Ally's care it seemed natural to let them be with him there as well. I couldn't have pried them loose with a crowbar anyway. They were stuck on him like little cockleburs. But I should have known that Allison and beer were a combination sure to inspire trouble.

I had put the other two children down for a nap in the afternoon and went in search of Alexanne and Mart for the same purpose. I knew they wouldn't go gladly, but it was going to be a long night of revelry and dancing, and I was determined we would all have a nap.

There was a group of cowboys under a stand of cottonwoods along the river, and I guessed that was where the beer would be. It didn't help to see Allison among the group, but it didn't surprise me either. What *did* surprise me was that Alexanne and Mart were at the center of the bunch, taking turns sipping off the cowboys' beer. The men thought it was cute as could be to initiate Ally's two young cowboys-in-training. They couldn't figure out why I flew into their midst and gave them all a good tongue mauling.

"It ain't as if it's whiskey, ma'am," one of the braver ones offered—like that made all the difference.

"Allison, I want to speak with you in private," I seethed. "And you two, get over to that tent and take the longest naps of your lives, do you hear?"

"Yes, Mama," they said, daunted. One thing I will say, they didn't have any trouble napping that afternoon.

Once I got Allison sequestered down-river a quarter mile, I really let him have it. I was so mad, tears were gushing out of my eyes.

"I cannot believe you would pull such a stunt! After what happened to Jack when he'd been drinking, and all of your own troubles with liquor! What in the world could you have been thinking?"

"I'm sorry, Josie. I never seem to do right by you."

"I'm not that hard to figure out, Allison. You know how I hate liquor! I hated it long before it played a part in Jack's death, and I will hate it till I die. You had no right to do that to my children."

"No, I didn't. I wasn't thinkin'. And I'm sorry."

"Sorry isn't enough, Allison. You will give them a lecture *yourself* on the sins of alcohol, and you will apologize to them—once they've sobered up."

"Yes, ma'am. I'll do whatever you think best."

"And let me tell you another thing. You have a choice to make, mister. If you want to be around your niece and nephews, you had better get used to the idea of staying sober, because I will not have one drop of liquor anywhere near them. Not ever again! Is that clear?"

"It is," he said, and I could see his soul retreating as resignedly as a turtle in its shell.

"Don't you dare misunderstand me, Allison Stewart! I've given you a choice, but you better understand that I'd rather have you around than gone!"

He looked at me, clearly surprised, a little skeptical.

"I don't know who it was in your life that gave you the idea that you're worthless, but I could skin the skunk alive. You're an amazing man! I've never seen anyone with such a plethora of talents. It hurts to know you've wasted them on cheap women and cards and liquor when you could have been teaching your niece and nephews all this time! They need you! Can't you see that?"

"I reckon I never looked at it that way."

"Well, they do! You are the only family they have. And they need your influence—I can't teach them to do the things you do. Nobody can but *you.* But they need you sober. I won't accept anything less."

He turned suddenly, got his horse, and rode off.

He didn't go so abruptly out of rudeness. He did it because he couldn't bear to have me see him in tears. It occurred to me, watching him go, that quite likely no one had ever given him such praise before. Never mind that it was delivered by such a stormy conveyance; it simply overwhelmed him.

I couldn't tell where he went. Nobody knew. I figured he had probably gone to town to defile himself and wondered at the brilliance of my praise. But when we got home, we found him there. The place was spotless. He had even mucked out the stable and moved the privy to a clean site.

But he had that look of apprehension whenever he glanced my way again, as if I were his singular figure of authority and he must live on eggshells in my presence for fear of displeasing me. It made me wonder what manner of neglect or abuse his father had wreaked on him as a child. And it made me angry at my father-in-law, even though I had never met the man.

By early August it was apparent that something had to be done to generate an income for the family. We still couldn't market our beef, and even though I kept a prolific garden, we would run short of food before winter was through. I managed to fend off disaster temporarily by selling a few head of cattle to the slaughterhouse.

Allison sold some of his horses, and made certain we always had fresh meat. He insisted it was his own stock he was butchering, but I knew he was beefing it. Given our circumstances, I couldn't argue with him, so I held my tongue and fed the children. As for me, I simply quit eating beef. I would eat the wild game he brought in—the antelope, elk, or venison—but I wasn't about to eat a steer that wasn't mine. I would rather have starved to death and flaunted my martyrdom in the cattlemen's faces than touch one ounce of their precious beef.

Then Whit told me about a teaching position the families along South Fork were offering. It was a nine-month job, starting in September.

They had the use of what was referred to as The Castle. Remnant of the early boom years, it had been the main ranch house of the huge English syndicate that had gone into receivership after the hard winter, and an imposing structure it was—by far the most ornate log home I ever saw. Two full stories tall, it was large enough for five families and decked out with the finest Victorian fixtures. It even had a hand-carved, black walnut banister and staircase imported from Europe. The kitchen was immense, designed to cook for a crowd. The English ranchers had entertained all manner of British and Continental aristocracy with ornate parties and hunting expeditions, which had been quite the rage in their time. I shudder to think of how many animals were slaughtered by those foreigners for trophy heads and skins alone, while American families across the plains starved for lack of being able to market their own cattle. I daresay we five families put The Castle to better use in nine months than the Brits did in all the years they claimed it.

Lest I convey the wrong idea, I should state that communal living—and with strangers, at that—was no picnic. Those nine months count as some of the more bizarre I have ever lived. If the choice had been mine, I would have shown a bit more discretion in picking the tenants.

I would have dispensed with the Maynards altogether. Never mind that they were secretive and surly, and of a class that was called white trash where I was born; I disliked them because they were gun people. The Sayers were poor and unschooled but amiable, and I didn't mind living with them. But between these two families there existed a combination that spelled trouble in capital letters: the Maynards had a fifteen-year-old son and the Sayers a daughter of fourteen, both of whom took to making eyes at one another straight off. The other two families were so quiet and retiring I can barely recall their names. One of them was Cleaver, but the other escapes me.

Not only did I teach school to all nineteen children in the Castle's oversized dining room, I cooked for the entire household. I know it sounds like a lot, and it was, but I did it by choice. You see, we lived in the kitchen and pantry—which itself was bigger than my bedroom at the homestead. And rather than have four other families stumbling around our living quarters, I arranged the have the others pay me to cook for the whole bunch. I was the only one experienced in cooking for a crowd, thanks to my tenure at mother's boarding house. They each paid an extra fifty-cents a week for my cooking services.

We hadn't been there more than two months when one evening after dinner, Mr. Sayer came in, mad as all get out. He rummaged around under the walnut stairway, pulled out his Winchester, and away he went. It didn't take long to determine that the Maynard boy had run off with his daughter. Once Sayer took off after them, old man Maynard took off after *him* armed with an arsenal, and the other two men figured they had better give chase to mediate.

That was a night I don't ever care to repeat. All of us women were on pins and needles, except Mrs. Maynard. We didn't know what she was doing or feeling. She had locked herself in her quarters.

They all returned at four in the morning. Sayer had shot the Maynard boy in the arm and got his daughter back. For some reason, old man Maynard had behaved himself and not fired a shot, though he was looking mighty irascible. I suspect the other men had made a threat that Maynard did not care to challenge.

We patched up young Maynard's wound, which didn't amount to more than a scratch, and I went out to the old bunkhouse to look up Frank Womac. Frank had worked for the Englishmen and somehow their disappearance hadn't put a dent in his loyalty to that ranch. He had elected himself caretaker, though no one had owned it or paid him for a number of years.

I told him what had happened and that while we women had awaited the outcome, we had taken a vote and decided the Maynards had to go. Naturally, the men agreed. Mr. Sayer concurred wholeheartedly, but we knew he in particular shouldn't confront them with the eviction. So I thought of Frank, since he was a neutral party and a rough old customer who wouldn't be intimidated by old man Maynard and his arsenal. And he *was* the caretaker, even if self-appointed. I think my request was the high point of Frank's decade. He grabbed his eight-gauge buckshot gun and motioned me to follow.

"You kin be the witness," he said.

We entered through the kitchen and could hear Mr. Sayer beating on the Maynards' door upstairs, demanding they come out. But they had locked themselves up tighter than Paradise.

Old Frank said nothing to Sayer, just swept him aside with a motion of the gun barrel. Frank had a gravelly voice that would sound scary to anyone who didn't know him.

"I'm gonna count to five," he said at the door. "If y'all ain't showed yer faces by the time six comes up, I'll have to open this door the hard way. And I want y'all to know it would put me in a real bad temper to have to ruin such a fine door with a load of buckshot."

He had counted up to four when the door came open just a sliver. We could see old man Maynard with a cocked pistol and his son backing him up with a rifle. Old Frank wasn't fazed a bit.

"You folks're gonna have to be cleared outta here in ten hours," he said.

"Who the hell do you think you are?" said Maynard.

"I'm caretaker of this outfit," Frank said. "And I've moved mightier men than you. Been all manner of shady characters wanted to set up housekeepin' here, and I reckon you don't notice any of 'em loiterin' around. And you just shortened your time to five hours fer cussin' in front of the ladies."

Maynard's eyes scanned the crowd. "We'll be gone," he grumbled, and closed the door.

They didn't make any more trouble. I have no idea where they went, but they were obviously adept at moving, because they were on their way before I had breakfast cooked. It may not seem neighborly to say it, but we were glad to be rid of them. Quite likely they moved on west, because we never heard of them in our country again.

Things went along pretty well after that. We settled into living more or less as one big family. Once the Maynard boy was gone, Barbara Sayer became quite an able student. She didn't seem to miss him, which gave me to believe that her father had done the right thing in going after her. Sometimes you can't tell which way a situation like that might turn.

Once winter hit, I sure missed my valley. The wind and cold out there on the plains were a tribulation. I marveled that I had ever weathered four winters on the Dakota plains. That time of my life seemed so distant then it was like looking back into someone else's memory.

About a month before school was out, our milk cow ran off. Frank sent Mart and Billy Cleaver after her, bareback, on an old cow pony of his named Ben. I was a little concerned, but Frank assured me that Ben was the best cow horse around. They found the milk cow, tangled up with a bunch of wild range stuff. Ben was doing a good job of separating the cow, but the first time he dodged a steer, he lost the boys. And Mart broke an arm.

Then they couldn't get back up on the horse. Finally Billy led Ben down a creek, backed him up to a bank and they managed to get aboard. And, wouldn't you know, they went and got that fool cow before they headed home, bless their dedicated little souls.

Mart's arm wasn't just broken, it was badly cut and bleeding. This excited the whole bunch of us women, and even obscured the fact that the arm was actually broken. I had him on the kitchen table trying to stem the flow of blood and sew it up while all the mothers and daughters hovered about attempting to make themselves useful. The scene amounted to a case of loosely organized hysteria, and I finally had to ask them to leave.

After several days Mart's wound healed, yet his arm remained swollen and so sore he wouldn't allow anyone touch him. When his fever spiked and sent him into fits of delirium, I finally determined the arm was broken. The break was up so far under the shoulder it was nearly impossible to diagnose. School would be over in two days, and I decided I would have to take him to a doctor immediately thereafter.

Gussie Fielder had come down to give us help in moving back

to the homestead. I had our wagon half-packed but decided the situation was grave enough that we should get to town as quickly as possible, so we chose to take her buckboard. One of her horses had wandered off during the night and I didn't think we should take time to look for it, so I went to see Frank Womac about borrowing one of his. That's when Mart went into such an animated fit of delirium he nearly caused a homicide.

He had been resting feverishly on his bed by the stove when somehow he got it into his head that there was a bunch of robbers in the house. So he leaped up and grabbed the first weapon he could find, which happened to be the meat saw. He was yelling and brandishing it around the kitchen trying to scare off the robbers when the Cleaver and Sayer girls came in and tried to subdue him. I guess he thought they were the culprits.

Alexanne came running for me, and by time I got there Mart had managed to capture Barbara Sayer and he was ready to start sawing. I felt mighty thankful just then that he hadn't found the butcher knife. Barbara was fifteen and not petite, so I perceived instantly that Mart was not merely crazy with delirium but in possession of that supernatural strength that can come with it.

It's amazing what a person will do in a crisis. I am uncertain whether it's a matter of pure reflex or if it's that precise moment when thought and action happen concurrently. I was still running into the room when I grabbed the water bucket and threw its contents on Mart, which brought him out of it. Barbara was surely happy to see me, even though she suffered a drenching. Up until that time all the girls in the house had had one gigantic crush on Mart. But he cured them all that day.

As if that situation hadn't been bad enough, once we were midway to town we managed to have a runaway. Gussie's horse resented being teamed with Frank's from the beginning.

The road ran right along the base of the mountains, and meandered up and down draws and among enormous boulders. Gussie, Alexanne, and I were on the seat, the boys in the back. Once the horses spooked and Gussie couldn't stop them, I took the reins and told her to grab Lex and the boys and scoot themselves to the rear end and roll off. Henry, ever fearful of feats of daring, instead rolled himself up in some blankets and hid under the seat. And Young Jack wasn't about to get off that buckboard without his Mother. He clung to the back of my skirt for dear life and got mad as the dickens at Martin, who was trying to pry him loose; all the while the buckboard went faster, jumping over rocks and virtually jarring the daylights out of us. Mart finally got some leverage and grabbed Jack and away they rolled. If I had known Henry was still under the seat, I probably would have stayed aboard and gone-down-with-the-ship and got my fool neck broken for it. Thinking everyone had gotten off, I finally jumped.

When the team eventually tore up the rig, Henry came out of it all right, but he was the only one who did. One horse was killed. Martin's arm—which had partially knit—broke again getting young Jack off the buckboard. Alexanne lit on her head and was out for twenty-four hours. The rest of us were scratched and bruised, but nothing too serious. It happened a few miles short of a settlement that served as a post office and stage stop, and there we managed to borrow a lumber wagon and continue toward town. We were really worried about Alexanne at that point, who was still out.

Mart could not get comfortable. We had him laid out in the bed of the wagon with Lex, but he thought that shoulder was going to kill him. So I brought him up on the spring seat with me, where the ride was less bumpy, and we drove all night. When we finally got to town Alexanne was coming to, but Mart's arm had swelled so badly the doctor couldn't do anything with it for more than a week, during which time it started knitting again.

When Doc Tessig and his nurse finally came around to our rented rooms to set it, he foolishly had Gussie handle the chloroform. Martin had been in and out of delirium, but he wasn't completely under when Doc went to work on the arm—which he had to re-break. Mart sat straight up and punched Doc square in the face with his good hand. At that point, Doc put a woman on each of Martin's legs and the good arm before he went back to work. It was a useless gesture, though, because Mart was out cold by then.

Doc never did come back to remove the splint. He told me when to take it off and how, and gave me a bill for seven dollars. And he did a good job. Mart never had another problem with that arm.

Seven dollars. Can you imagine? I guess he didn't see fit to charge anything extra for that punch in the nose.

It was while we were in town waiting for Mart's swelling to abate that I heard about the Myers Hotel. It was a small boarding house with a large public restaurant, and it was for lease. I knew it was a business I could manage efficiently, and though I did not hanker to live in town, our experiences on the plains had given me the notion that living so remotely while the children were growing had its disadvantages. I could make far more money on the Hotel than teaching or ranching, most of which I could save, and the children could go to school in town. In those days when there were so few rural schools, it was not unusual for families to send their children into town for the school term anyway. Many of the wealthy ranchers maintained homes in town for that purpose and for the convenience of living less remotely during the harsh winter months.

The children pitched a loud protest. They didn't want to become town sissies, but I assured them it was temporary—four years at the most—then we would go back to the homestead with money to back us up against the kind of circumstances that had landed us there in the first place.

Whit finally got word of the accident and came to get Gussie. He thought the Hotel was a splendid idea, and offered to bring in our wagon and belongings.

So I was back in the boarding house business.

The restaurant was the real moneymaker, though. I saw to it that we had the best menu around, and that assured us of a constant clientele. When the cowboys and range-hands found out, they made it a point to patronize our establishment whenever they were in town—and there were *always* cowboys in town. And, in spite of the cattlemen's efforts to the contrary, I finally had my own market for my beef.

Allison watched the livestock and the homestead in the summer months and wintered with us in town. His cough was constant by then, and he simply could not work outside in cold weather. Winters, Whit took over with the livestock and the homestead and Allison did odd jobs around the Hotel. But winter, summer, spring, or fall, there was a constant flow of cowboys at the restaurant.

It started with Whit and Allison, then Billy Shaw and Ben Lattis. Right from the beginning, one of them would make a late evening visit every week or so. And after they came, there was always fresh meat hanging in the restaurant's pantry. Then other men, mostly friends whose faces I recognized, would bring in the beef, saying it was sent by Allison or Whit from the homestead. Even the occasional ones I didn't recognize always seemed more than glad to do a favor for Jack Stewart's widow,

At the end of the first year, when I sat down with Whit for a report on my range stock, I was surprised to find that I had considerably more beef on the hoof wandering the range than I had started with that year.

"How can that be, Whit?" I asked.

"It's a well-known fact, Josie, that cows'll have calves every spring," he said all-too-innocently.

"That's not what I mean, and you know it. By my count, seventeen of my steers have been butchered for the restaurant, and yet you say those seventeen are still wandering the range in addition to the new calf crop."

"Yes, they are," he said matter-of-factly.

I eyed him. "Then precisely whose beef have my customers been eating for the last six months?"

He twiddled his thumbs and looked at the corner of the room evasively. "I couldn't say for sure."

I rose to my feet. "Whit Fielder, are you telling me that I have unwittingly been made a party to the sale and consumption of stolen beef?"

"Sit down, Josie."

"No. Answer me."

"Josie, sit down," he said seriously.

I sat down, but remained staring. "It's stolen, isn't it?"

"I wouldn't say it is or isn't," he intoned. "But I will tell you this: Whatever it is, you are to regard it as an insurance policy."

I leaped to my feet. "I will not accept stolen beef. You know better than to attempt such a thing!"

He stood, facing me. "Sit down, Josie."

We both sat down, staring each other eye for eye.

"Now, you listen to me," he said. "I know you don't want to hear this, and I would have preferred not to say it, but we can't avoid it now. You are not to ask whose beef comes through this pantry, do you hear? But it will come, and even I couldn't tell you the names of all the men intent on bringing it. I can't tell you whose beef it's been the last six months or whose it'll be in the future, but I will tell you whose it *won't* be. Not one head of Jack Stewart's stock will be butchered for this restaurant. I think you know why, but I'm gonna tell you anyway. You have been violently robbed of your husband and your children of their father. If this is the only way the perpetrators will pay for that murder, then by the gods, so be it. They *will* pay, Josie. And you will not argue."

"Do you realize that some of those men are customers at this restaurant?"

"All the better. I favor a touch of irony along with my beef —adds to the flavor, don't you think?"

"This goes against everything Jack believed. He would never have allowed this, Whit, and you know it."

"Yes, I do know that, Josie. And if Jack were alive right now we wouldn't have need of this conversation, would we? They did more than cross the bounds of ethics, Mrs, Stewart. They murdered decent men—one of whom was your husband and one of whom was our closest friend."

We stared at each other. "I'll never eat a bite of it," I said stonily.

"That's your prerogative," said Whit. "But don't you dare refuse it. This is our only chance at justice, and we are determined to see it through."

In all the years I ran that Hotel, never once did I buy a side of beef. And never once did a morsel of the abundant beef that appeared in the pantry ever cross my lips. At that point I quit eating meat altogether on sheer principle and took up Dr. Trall's Hygienic System of diet.

I have never understood fully why Whit and Billy pressed Allison to leave the country. Although it was at times a tribulation having him around the Hotel—not just because of his cough but because he would inevitably start drinking in earnest by January—I wouldn't have gone so far as to push him out of the country. But Whit took me aside, asking me once again not to argue.

"But he's sick, Whit. I doubt he's got more than five years left in him."

"He knows that, Josie. We all do."

"Then how can you ask him to leave? As much of a nuisance as he can be, he has his qualities. And he's still family, and I'm obligated to take care of him."

"That's part of the problem. Hardly anyone but us fellas who growed up with 'em knows that Ally is Jack's brother. Allison's been careful to maintain that, because he wouldn't ever want to embarrass you by family connection. But people are starting to talk. After, all, he's here at the Hotel in winter with the kids callin' him Uncle, and we reckoned things was gettin' a little close for comfort. Then, too, there's been some talk among the wrong crowd of that murder warrant again, and we'd like to avoid any more range violence. We're finally getting on speakin' terms instead of shootin' terms, and nobody wants to upset the possibility of peace. It's too delicate a balance just yet. We've all got to tread softly. Both sides. It'll take years to settle the issue as it is."

"I sense you're not telling me the whole story, Whit."

He smiled. "You always were a bit too perceptive. No, there is one other thing. We both know that Allison can be less than discreet at times. Some of our boys told me they saw a Herman brand still visible on a beef Ally was bringin' in to the restaurant not long ago."

"Are you going to pretend you haven't done the same thing? Whit, I never figured you for a hypocrite. How can you talk to me about peace negotiations and disparage Allison for beefing while you all are doing the same thing?"

"I won't defend or deny—you already know my position. And peace negotiations have nothing to do with that insurance policy. But discretion does. And it's precisely because of Allison's lack of discretion that he could endanger both your insurance policy *and* the negotiation."

"I won't even attempt to understand that. You're starting to sound like a politician, and that scares me."

He laughed. "I'm not asking you to understand it, Josie. I'm only asking that you don't argue. Ally has to go. He's jeopardizing your safety, and we simply can't have that."

"If he weren't sick, I could take this better. I don't feel right pushing him away. People have done that to him too much in his life."

"Don't think of it as pushing him away. I've talked to Ally and he wants to go. Besides, you know as well as I do that he'd shoot himself before he'd let any of us take care of him for one hour as an invalid—especially you."

Two days later Allison left. He didn't say good-bye. His illness would probably have made him too emotional for any farewells with the children. But he wrote them all a note, telling them good-bye and giving them each a horse. He deeded to me his homestead, his cattle, and the rest of the horses—except his favorite called White Man, which he took with him when he headed north.

A year later I received a letter. I sat on the back stoop off the kitchen in the rich light of late afternoon, unaware that tears were creeping down my face. The children were coming up the alleyway from school and stopped when they saw me.

"What's the matter, Mama?" said Alexanne.

I motioned for them and they settled about me, concerned.

"I got a letter today," I said, "from a nice doctor up in Montana. He had been treating Uncle Ally for awhile, and recently diagnosed him with consumption."

"What's that?" asked Young Jack.

"It's a lung disease, honey. It's what made him cough so much."

Mart looked at me, knowing. "Has he got sicker, Mama?"

"No, son. Your Uncle Allison is dead."

They all stared. Alexanne was the first to find words. "How, Mama? Did the consumption kill him?"

"No. Once that young doctor diagnosed him, he walked out to the street just like he knew exactly where he was going. He picked a gunfight with a cowboy and never fired a shot at him. He just let that young man kill him."

Tears were unanimous now. Mart looked plaintively at me. "Did they hang the fella who kilt him?"

"No, son. Too many people saw it, and they all agreed it was more or less self-defense. And you know Uncle Ally—he wouldn't have wanted that poor man to go to jail for it. He wanted to die,"

"Why, Mama?" said Alexanne. "Why did he want to die? I would've taken care of him when he got sick."

"I know, honey. We all would have. But Uncle Allison, you see, he just couldn't let people take care of him. He was determined about it."

"Why, Mama?" said Henry, his head in my lap.

"He just didn't think he deserved it, son. He just didn't think he was worth anyone's attention."

"But he was!" Mart said staunchly. "He was a good man. I know he drank too much, and gambled, but that don't mean he wasn't a good man. He was!"

"Yes, he was in his fashion. And that's what he would want us all to remember him for. All the good things—how strong he was, and tough. Remember when he had that horse wreck and was torn up and how he never cried? And how good he was at teaching you to be cowboys and wranglers."

"He was the best, Mama," said Mart.

I nodded. "Yes, sir. Allison was special."

He was what my grandson would have called a "cowboy deluxe." He was the only man we ever knew who could rope anything on anything.

CHAPTER TEN
THE ROAN MAVERICK
(And Other Stories)

I t had taken the good doctor's letter so many weeks to reach me that Allison was long buried in a pauper's grave by the time I knew of his death. Evidently he and the doctor had struck up a friendship during the course of his treatment. The physician knew there was a younger sister in Texas and somehow managed to contact Leigh, asking if she would like shipped to her Allison's only possessions—his horse, saddle, and guns. Due to the expense, she declined, and informed the doctor that my family was closer and might like to have them. By the time he wrote to me, White Man had been sold to pay the undertaker. I sent the doctor enough money to cover the cost of shipping the saddle and Winchester to me, and asked him to keep the pistol as a token of their friendship and in appreciation for the trouble he had gone to on the family's behalf.

Allison's death seemed to symbolize the end of an era for me. He represented the most proficient and was one of the last of the old-time cowboys, the true open range cowboys. The business of ranching had been in the throes of change long before he died, the invasion being the most extreme manifestation of that change. Even though the cattlemen had gone to war to protect their monopoly on free government grass, it was apparent that the open range system was not a particularly efficient means by which to run a cattle operation—at least not as it was practiced by the large cattle concerns. Out of necessity, we small ranchers had had to be more efficient, especially given the market tyranny, and were accustomed to the rigors of economizing. And our herds were smaller and therefore more manageable.

All this time the big outfits had run their cattle free on the range and had, for the greater part, not even bothered to stake legal claims on their home ranches. Never mind that this gave them virtually no water rights; what mattered to the managers of these large corporations was that they didn't have the responsibility of owning and managing any of the land they were using. They had free grass, and they used book count to tally their herds, which was inexact at best and allowed them to project assets to the corporate stockholders they all too often did not have. In tallying by book count, a rancher measured his herd by the supposition that for every calf branded at round-up he had fifteen head of grown stock on the range. The likelihood of mismanagement in such a deceptive environment was virtually guaranteed. The hard winter of 1886-7 had toppled many a mismanaged corporation and was the harbinger of the end of the open range cow business.

There were cattlemen who, after the fiasco of the invasion, recognized the inevitability of change and began to adapt. Gil Herman was one of the first to convert to the fenced-and-managed system in our country, and to acquire resource rights through the Desert Land and Homestead Acts. Arthur Adams was another.

Mr. Adams had almost been one of the invaders. He had, in fact, met them the night prior to their attack on Will's place. But when he found out what they planned to do, he delivered them a sermon that would have made a preacher cringe, then stormed out. For years the invaders called him a coward behind his back. Jimmy Bovin actually had the audacity to call him that to his face—right on the main street of town—to which Adams staunchly replied, "It took a better man to leave that outfit than any one of you who stayed with it." When that statement made the rounds of the county, most of the cowboys who had decried Adams for attempting to join the invaders began changing their tune and the other cattlemen ceased bothering him.

I always liked Arthur Adams, not because he and his wife came from cultivated eastern backgrounds, but because they were unusual as ranchers. Unlike most of the big outfits, which were corporate-owned and managed by people like Herman or Bovin, Adams ran his as a sole proprietor. And he lived on his ranch with his family—another rarity. Granted, he sent his five children east for their higher learning, but by the time every one of them left for school they were westerners to the core and property owners by homestead—even the three girls, two of whom showed inventive cleverness in acquiring their property. They claimed adjoining acreage, and rather than build two homestead cabins, built one structure smack on the joint property line. My grandson called them "cowgirls deluxe," and they were women worthy of the title. Their older sister, who was beautiful and brainy and had been appointed State Librarian right out of college, went on to become my grandson's mother—my daughter-in-law, Angeline Adams Stewart.

Some people found it maddening and too ironic that the son of a murdered settler and the daughter of a wealthy cattleman could even consider marriage. But Martin and Angeline were willing victims of love-at-first-sight, and a finer match was never made. If she had been the daughter of Herman or Bovin, I might have objected. But I had no quarrel with Arthur Adams.

It took two more years than planned to move back to the homestead. The restaurant was so lucrative it was hard to give it up, and I was determined to never be without money again. So I extended my lease and banked every extra penny, hoping someday to send my children to college.

Mart could never quite acclimate to life in town, and when Whit offered to take him back out to the valley as a ranch hand, I agreed on the condition that Martin continue his schooling whenever the rural term was in session. Whit was glad to have an able hand. He had two sons, but they were just little boys and Gussie was prone to spoiling them something awful. Mart was so much like Jack, I think it gave Whit the vicarious sense of being with his old boyhood pal again.

Around that time, Whit decided someone should carry on in

the Jack Stewart Tradition and challenge the market restrictions openly. He was becoming quite well-thought-of in the community and had made it a point to establish a business relationship with the local banker—whose interests ran quite heavily toward the white cap persuasion, and who in 1895 was our newly-elected state representative. When it came time for the legislative session, Whit handed banker Jeffers a bill for fifteen hundred dollars.

"I'd like you to take that down to the Livestock Commissioners, if you would, James, and present it for collection," Whit said. "It's a tally of the cost of the livestock I've had seized over the past few years."

"Whit, I don't believe I could do that," Jeffers said.

"Yes, I believe you can, James. You're our elected representative, and it's your solemn duty to represent us. This is an issue that needs addressing, and I believe you're the man to do it. That's why I voted for you. The only alternative, as I see it, would be to get all these little outfits together and file a civil suit against the State and the Livestock Commissioners. It's occurred to a few of us that the United States Supreme Court might like to hear such a case."

Jeffers smiled appreciatively. "I'll see what I can do for you, Whit. But I won't make any guarantees."

When Jeffers returned, he handed Whit a check for fifteen hundred dollars and a lifelong friendship was born. Within a year, thanks in part to Whit's action and some fine editorials by John Burgee, the legislature passed a resolution granting inspection privileges to *all* registered brands and the market tyranny was finally over.

Somewhere around the turn of the century, Billy Shaw sold his interest in the Boot Five and moved to the more temperate climate of California. Mart grew up working for Whit's Powderhorn and the Boot Five. We hadn't known Ben Lattis too well up to that point.

Even though he had always been a part of our group, Ben was a one-directed and frugal sort who preferred to be working hard at turning a profit rather than talking. He had not one ounce of tolerance for the cattlemen and their shenanigans. I think he despised them even more deeply than I did. While the rest of the group had pretty much buried the hatchet by 1900, Ben Lattis was relentless. Once I quit the restaurant business, there was little reason for the men to continue beefing. But I don't think Ben ever gave up killing Yankton stock.

When Mart was thirteen and a regular ranch hand with Whit and Ben, someone came to them with word that Ed Weston was coming into town on the stage. He hadn't been seen anywhere near our country since the invasion. The last anyone had heard he was up in the Klondike with the gold rush. Because of his crimes and his cowardly disappearance, our boys pretty much felt that if Weston ever showed his face in our country they would be obliged to kill him. When the news came, Whit and Ben wasted no time fixing for the ride to town. They put Mart on a horse, too, stuck a pistol in his belt, and insisted that he personally meet that stage. Somehow, Whit and Ben had convinced Mart that it was his duty to confront the man who had murdered his father and shoot the skunk dead. I am sure Mart was also remembering my hideous pronouncement that I was going to "raise my son to kill Ed Weston."

Can you imagine the emotional stress this must have placed on a thirteen- year-old boy? I will never forgive myself or Whit and Ben for doing such a thing to him.

Mart told me later that as much as he feared Ed Weston, he was petrified of what Whit and Ben might do if he didn't live up to the deed, so he braced himself and met the stage. Whit and Ben had coached him. He was to step up to Weston as soon as he alighted and say, "I'm the son of the man you murdered," and pull his gun.

What Mart didn't know is that Whit and Ben planned to do the actual killing. I suppose the whole performance was meant to not only make Weston confront the son of his victim, but to teach Mart some sort of manly comportment. I know life was rougher in those days, but this was taking things way too far. If I had had any knowledge of what Whit and Ben were up to, I would have given them both a good scalding.

As fate would have it, Weston abruptly left the stage many miles south of town at Powder River Crossing. Whether this happened out of clairvoyance on Weston's part or the probability that the ghosts of Jackson Stewart and Will Standifer made Powder River country too uncomfortable for him, I couldn't say. It's unlikely that anyone warned him of what was afoot, but whatever his reason I'm glad he slunk away. Thankfully, Mart was spared the confrontation. I shudder to think of what may have happened if it had taken place. I may well have lost Mart to Weston, too. I might have expected that type of stunt from Ben Lattis, unforgiving and stern as he was, but what Whit Fielder could possibly have been thinking, I will never understand. Thankfully, Weston never came back again.

In later years, Mart would say he felt certain it was Gil Herman who sent the messenger to Whit and Ben with the news of Weston's arrival. Even Whit hinted on more than one occasion that he suspected Weston had been attempting to blackmail Herman for years and was coming to collect. I couldn't verify that, but it would not surprise me. By then Herman had put as much distance between his own reputation and Weston's as possible.

Mart was not quite sixteen when Ben and Whit made him brand the roan maverick. In the spring of 1903 there were very few cattle in the Salt creek country that didn't belong to Whit or the Boot Five. And, naturally, in a big country some calves were missed in the round-up, so they were branding up the stuff that had been missed the previous fall. By then—though on a much smaller scale— working the range had gotten to be much the way it had been before everything got tangled up in the Maverick Laws. Any calf would be branded for the cow it belonged to, and the big unmarked calves were branded for the outfits working the round-up. By that time there were more small outfits than big ones participating, and quite often the little outfits would pool together on a wagon. Mavericks older than long yearlings had all but disappeared from the range. There were fewer cattle, for one thing, and the stock that existed was managed better than the enormous herds of the 1880s. The Boot Five had a wagon, which Whit shared, so when Whit and Ben were divvying up mavericks, they would brand one for the Boot Five and one for the Powderhorn. They were out on Hay Draw that spring of 1903 when they spied a big roan maverick running with a bunch of long yearlings.

Ben looked at Whit and they both looked at Mart.

"Did we ever give you anything, son?" said Ben.

"Yessir, you give me my wages once a year," Mart replied.

Whit smiled. "But we never cut out a maverick for you."

"No, sir."

"Well, right there is probably the last four year old slick-sided steer that'll ever be seen on this range. He's all yours, Mart. Ride out there and brand him."

Mart looked at the maverick then at the men. He was riding Old Billy, who was an awful good horse in a cow hunt, but he wasn't much of a horse at roping. Mart knew Old Billy would want to get up there and try to herd that steer, and he would be fighting the horse the whole time, and probably get jerked down in the process. He knew I wouldn't approve of him branding a maverick, even though the offer came from its rightful owners. He knew his father would not have approved—and his Uncle Allison would not have hesitated. And he knew, the principle of the thing and Old Billy to the contrary, the two men on either side of him would accept nothing less than seeing him brand that maverick.

Because he perceived it as primarily a symbolic gesture, he swallowed his fear and rode out there. Fighting Old Billy the whole way, he roped that big roan maverick, tied it down, built his sagebrush fire and branded it. It was the first and last maverick to ever wear Martin Stewart's brand, and the last known steer on the range to live four years unmarked.

Martin married Angeline in 1915. By then he was twenty-eight and Whit Fielder's partner in the Powderhorn. They did well until the drought and hard winter of 1919, which nearly put us all under. That was the year Joe was born.

When Mart found out Angeline was expecting, he was happy

as a basket of puppies. They had decided their first child would be named Joseph Jackson Stewart, after me and Jack. All during the gestation Mart would grin and say things like, "When Joe gets here, I won't have to get down off my horse to open a gate"; or, "By golly, when Joe gets here he can give me a hand with them horses"; or, "When Joe gets here we can finally fence that upper pasture."

When Joe got there he was a bouncing baby girl named Josephine Jackson Stewart. But she was Joe before she arrived and she remained Joe all her life. And she lived up to every ranching expectation Mart ever had. She was the only female foreman I never knew—and I mean foreman of a big outfit. That was after Martin retired from the Sheriff's Department and was managing a large Canadian cattle company on South Fork of Powder River.

Lex would have sure been proud of her.

Mart and young Jack were the only two of my children who survived past 1920. I lost Henry to the Great War. They buried him somewhere in France. He was such a gentle soul, bright and serene, and the only one of my children to ever go to college. Alexanne married a rancher from Washington State and was expecting their first child when the influenza epidemic took them all. Young Jack never married. He was always a loner, much like Allison, and remained a bachelor cowboy all his life. So it was left up to Mart to carry on the family name. After Joe, Mart and Angeline had my grandsons, Thomas Allison and Arthur Adams. All three grandchildren graduated college.

There weren't many of the men from our group who made it past 1930. Billy Shaw and Ben Lattis did, but most of the others were gone by then. Whit died in 1925. He was a state senator then, had been in politics for a number of years. He was killed in an automobile accident with his friend, the banker-politician James Jeffers. They were on their way to the capital when Jeffers' car went out of control and rolled into a gully.

Angeline died in an auto accident in 1940.

Mart was diagnosed with cancer in 1950. That was the same year we heard from Leigh in Texas and decided to visit her. I had no idea any of Jack's family would still be alive. I was ninety years old then and, remarkably, in better health than my own son. To this day, I contend I owe my longevity to the adoption of Dr. Trall's Hygienic System—you can't seem to go wrong with plain old fruits, grains, and vegetables.

It was during Martin's illness and just prior to the trip to Texas that his children, Joe and Tom, decided to invest in the most up-to-date technological device to record the family history. They bought, at what I considered an enormous expense, a tape recorder. It was a cumbersome thing that weighed a ton and used two big reels that ate up miles and miles of tape. Now I can appreciate their foresight, but at the time I thought they were spending an awful lot of money on something that could easily have been supplanted with some good old-fashioned pencils, paper, and elbow grease. But I listen to those tapes now and have to smile at hearing Martin's voice as if he were sitting right here next to me.

It was on the trip to Texas that we gave the tape recorder its maiden run. Leigh and her granddaughter met us at the train station in Austin and she commented straight off how much Martin looked like her brother Allison and how much young Tom looked like Jack. She was in her eighties and, though a shy, retiring woman, was game for telling the early years of the Stewart family history as best she could remember it.

She took us out to the sight of the old family ranch, where she showed us the graves of her parents and grandparents. Then on tape she told the story of how her grandfather was killed by Comanches on the same hunting expedition when Mr. Wilbarger was scalped—he was the only one of the party who lived, albeit without his topknot.

She brought out all the old family pictures, mostly daguerreotypes and tintypes. It was strangely unsettling to see Jack and Allison as youngsters, staring at me from the silvered surfaces of those tiny metal plates. If the light hit them just right, the image looked ethereally three-dimensional. It was apparent that Jack favored their father's side of the family—light-complected and ambitious—while Allison favored their mother's. She had been a dark-haired, dark-eyed beauty, quiet and vaguely mysterious. This difference in appearance made it easy for the boys to hide their familial connection all those years up north.

Leigh showed us a copy of the open letter the head of the Texas Masons wrote to the Wyoming Governor and the stock association when Jack was killed. News of the troubles up there was nationwide, and when the Association attempted to insinuate that Jack was a cattle thief, the Masons got involved, denouncing the stockmen for attempting to debase the reputation of such a respectable, educated family man.

Leigh told what she could remember of growing up with her two older brothers. Jack was twelve years her senior and had left for college when her memories began in earnest. And even though Allison had pretty much grown up on his own working cattle out in the brush, his image was clear in her mind. He had been her friend and protector, walking her to and from school when the Olive gang was stirring up trouble in McDade, escorting her back and forth between their step-mother's house and the homes of their dead mother's sisters. I gathered from the way she spoke there was some ill feeling between the sisters and the step-Mrs. Stewart.

I showed her photographs of Jack and Ally from the days of the cattle war, formal sittings they had had taken in town and round-up pictures taken by traveling photographers. She recognized Jack immediately but remarked with surprise on how different Allison was. "He looks so fierce!" she said. "He never had that fierce look in all the years I knew him."

It was during Mart's protracted illness, which kept him abed much of his last months, that the tape recorder really came in handy. Practically everyone in our country knew Mart from his twenty years as sheriff—and, where the old cowboys were concerned, as Jack Stewart's son.

When he had been sheriff, the old-timers would congregate

in his office after five o'clock and tell stories of the cattle war. This was where Joe and Tom had gotten their interest in the family history. They would meet their father at his office after school and inevitably ended up sitting on the laps of the old cowboys as the stories unfolded around the pot-bellied stove.

So when Mart got sick with the cancer, Joe and Tom invited all the old-timers who were still living to visit him and tell their stories again while the tape recorder rolled. As old as those men were and as sick as Mart was, it was surprising how none of them ever forgot that tape recorder. And when they wanted to tell something that was not for publication, they would look at Joe or Tom and say, "Turn 'er off for just a minute."

Many of the men who came were Martin's contemporaries and had worked for him or with him, and some were the sons of the old-time cowboys like he was. Their memories ran more to anecdotes of cowboy life after the turn of the century, or Prohibition and Depression stories. I found these tales as interesting as the cattle war stuff, and marvel whenever I listen to these tapes at what a wonderful chronicle they are of life on the northern plains. I can also see in retrospect how growing up in an atmosphere of terror had shaped the lives of many of these men. They were tough as nails. They worked hard and played rough—as you can see from this excerpt:

"Here the other day we were talkin' about how Mart didn't want to take any of those pills till it was necessary. One time when he was down on the Powderhorn, he had a pretty good young man workin' for him and something happened and this fella hurt himself. Mart was tryin' to get a lot of work done before winter set in and he didn't want to stop. This young fella was complainin' a bit and Mart said, 'Oh, we don't pay attention to little things like that out here.' So the kid gritted his teeth and stayed with him. They was puttin' on a head gate for an irrigation ditch and Mart was out there in the river up to his waist in that icy water. They was pryin' this log around to drop it in place and it was wet and slippery, and when it come over, it come down on Mart's hand. Took the hide off the back of it—skin was hangin' down over his fingers like an apron. It sure hurt, but

he remembered tellin' this young fella that they didn't stop for hurts so he had to keep on till he finished the job. When they were ridin' back down to the ranch, this fella had been watchin' Mart and he knew his hand was hurtin' him awful bad. He said, 'I don't know what it would take to hurt a fella around here so he'd be crippled enough to quit workin' for the day. Do you reckon if you died work would go on just the same'?"

(Laughter)

Mart: "I remember him. He was from Nebraska, and a sight more well-behaved than this group of local kids I'd have workin' every fall. Course, there was just too much daylight that time of year and these kids'd get to feelin' too good. Remember Ol' Hampshire? He was all the time shootin' off his head, gettin' in trouble with the kids. They just loved to jump him and really get rough whenever they had the chance. And he'd holler to get them kids off him—and you could hear him holler 'Mart!' for a mile, you know. One time just before dark he come to me and said, 'Them kids, I'm afraid they're gonna kill me this time.' And I said, 'Go over to the cook tent, Hamp, and sit in there. Get you a short club that you can handle and don't be backward about hittin' 'em.' So he went in there and got a stick of wood so big he could barely grip it with both hands. And pretty soon here come the kids. There was about six of 'em. You was in on that, Pete."

Pete: "Yessir. Me and Riley and the Fielder boys."

Mart: "I had an axe handle that I carried to fend you boys off, 'cause you'd jump any of us men. I snuck into the corner of the tent and set there. I forgot the name of that one fella we had along, but he was kinda dumb and we just had him drivin' the bed wagon. He was always sittin' around where he didn't belong, and he had squatted down in that tent. When you kids come at us, I swung at Riley and missed. Hit that other fella right between the eyes with the nubbin' end of that axe handle, and he just fell over. Then I got some action on Riley and managed to whack his shin. He had a swolled-up leg for half the winter. The Fielder boys was on Ol' Hamp, and once I got past you and Riley, I took them on. That just tickled Hamp to death. He used to brag how he never had any more trouble with you boys after I got rough with you. He'd say somethin' smart and maybe tie into you kids when he didn't have a chance in the world. He got several beatin's. 'Course, once in a while I got a pretty good lickin' too."

THE ROAN MAVERICK

Pete: "Yeah, we used to treat you fellas purty rough. By gosh, though, I always kicked myself—you know that time we was down there at the Cowan water gap on that cactus flat? Well, we got into it there. I was after Old Hampshire and Austin Fielder was after you. You and Austin was wrestlin' and I had Hamp so that all I'd have to done was give him a push and he'd've lit in the biggest ol' cactus bed you ever seen. And I didn't have the nerve. Just couldn't do it. And then I looked up, and you had ol' Austin there, jest a-jammin' his head up and down in a cactus bed."

(Laughter)

Joe: "Dad, tell the story about Ben Lattis's cook."

Mart: "Racehorse Frenchy? He was the dirtiest thing you ever saw. He never did take off a pair of overalls. They just commenced to rot out underneath and come apart, you know, and he'd finally take the waist band off. My land, he was dirty. Bein' such a penny pincher I think Ben kinda liked havin' Frenchy around, cuz nobody'd freeload off our cook wagon with someone that dirty workin' the food. Ben use to tell folks, 'If you ever watched that man cook, you'd give up eatin' and starve to death.' That last ship we had him on we pulled in to the Gilbertson water gap with a bunch of cows and bedded down. Generally, from there Ben'd go on into town and let me bring 'em in myself. I was just a kid, but I could handle it from there alright with our other men. Once Ben left, we was figurin' how we could get rid of Frenchy. Besides bein' so dirty you lost your appetite, he couldn't cook worth a darn. So that evenin' a couple of boys decided to scare him off, and they got Frenchy, tied him up like a mummy, and took him down to the river and made like they was gonna drown him. They was makin' it so realistic ol' Frenchy couldn't get it through his head they wasn't serious, and he pert'near got to prayin' and beggin'. He confessed he wasn't no cook; he'd only taken the job cuz his racehorse was mortgaged. But he said if the boys'd untie him, he'd leave. So they let him up and he turned in his pot-hook. Ben never could figure out why Frenchy quit. Course, that little job backfired on me cuz I was left to do the cookin'."

(Laughter)

Dahl: "Frenchy sounds like ol' Clifford Clark. He was cookin' out at the pool wagon. Gosh, he was dirty. If he couldn't find a towel, he'd just blow his nose in his hand and give a little throw and go on makin' biscuits."

(Groans and laughter)

Pete: *"Mart, do you remember the time you throwed me in the waterhole? I believe it was the summer of 1915 and I was wranglin' horses for Daddy Burnett."*

Mart: *"Yeah."*

Pete: *"We was camped about a half mile east of Trabin' on that long cactus flat. There was a big waterhole there, that's where the mess tent and wagons was. You cowboys made a short circle that mornin' and you got in kinda early. It was an awful hot day and you all decided to go down to the creek and take a swim. I had the horses a little way from camp, and I could see you down there. And I seen these little piles of clothes along the bank, and a pair of boots along each one. So I conceived the idea that it'd be mighty funny if I'd go and take a boot from each pile and then watch you boys hop towards camp across that cactus flat. So, when you all got down underneath the bank out of sight, I galloped up fast as I could and hopped off my horse and run along, tryin' to get a boot from each pile of clothes. And you fellas saw me and you started chuckin' rocks at me. I was a-dodgin' rocks and grabbin' boots as I ran. Then I went and dropped all these boots over at the camp and rode out to the horse cavvy. It sure was funny to watch you hoppin' along tryin' to dodge cactus, and I just laughed and laughed. Well, purty soon I had to bring the horses in so you could make your afternoon circle, and I begin to get uneasy. It wasn't so funny then, knowin' I had to face you all. You fellas was eatin' dinner, so I throwed the horses in the rope corral and got my food. I noticed all you cowboys eyein' me. And I didn't like the way you looked at me. Soon as you was through eatin', George and you grabbed me by the arms and feet and took me out to that big waterhole. You swung me back and forth several times, and I thought, 'They're just tryin' to scare me; they ain't gonna throw me in that deep muddy water.' Then all at once you give me a big heave and out I went, right into the middle. I sunk down, then finally come up sputterin' mud, and I hear you say, 'Steal our boots, will you!' and you figured that taught me a lesson. But I thought, I'm gonna get even with those men. So a few days later, we was camped south of there and one evenin' I was comin' in from the horses and I run across a*

148

porcupine. So I hazed this crittur up toward the mess tent where you fellas was playin' poker and got him in there without you all knowin'. Purty soon I hear someone say, 'For the love of Mike, would you look there?—there's a porcupine!' And I hollers, 'Throw me in that waterhole, will you?' Well, soon as you hazed that porcupine out of there, you fellas grabbed me and one set on my head and one on my feet and you chapped me good. I could hardly sit a horse for a week. That's when I figured out there was no use tryin' to get even with a big bunch of fellas, cuz they could always get one up on you."

(Laughter)

Dahl: "By gosh, we got one over on Mart once. He was up there havin' a big conflab with Ben, and he was in the house for two, three hours. Austin and me was just sittin' around, so we slipped down to that old Ford Mart had. That's when the gas tank was under the seat. You had to have quite a bit of gravity to feed it. So I snuck around there and shut off the gas. Pretty soon Mart come out and he got down to the Ford and cranked it and cranked it. Walked around that thing and cranked it some more. Ben come out and cranked it. Austin cranked it—"

Mart: "Oh, you used to make it a point to get one over on me or make off with whatever you could lift from me. He made off with several saddle ropes and a pair of stirrups. And course I was stealin' things back off him as fast as I could, but he didn't never have too much worth stealin'. But finally I got ahold of a good sweater, best sweater I ever seen, thick tight wool—coat sweater, you know. I had to watch it pretty close, but I managed to wear it out. So I figured I got the best of it."

Dahl: "I'd forgotten that."

Mart: "Best sweater I ever owned."

Dahl: "What do you mean, owned?"

Pete: "Say, did I hear that Billy Shaw died?"

Mart: "Yes, Billy's dead."

Pete: "California?"

Mart: "Yeah. He come down through here a couple times. Went all over the country here, wanted to see some of the old places."

Pete: "You was awful young when you started workin' for them at Fielders and the Boot Five, wasn't you?"

Mart: "When I started I guess I was about eight years old. Pert'near *have to put me on my horse. We just had a pack outfit for years up there. Then we graduated to a buggy and then a wagon. There was no mess box on it, just some boxes throwed in there. I started as horse wrangler and then I never did get away from that wagon. I never got to go out for reppin', because if a cook quit, I was cook. Night hawk quit, I was night hawk. And the rest of the time I was punchin' cows. When I was sixteen, they were gonna turn the wagon over to me, but they were afraid I might have some trouble with those ol' reps from the outside. Might get some cranky ol' bird who might run me out. So I didn't get the wagon then, but in one day I could be wrangler plumb up to boss. A bunch of those old fellas, they wouldn't wrangle and they wouldn't night hawk, so I had the best education of the lot of 'em."*

Dahl: "Those Yankton hands, by golly, they was darn picky about what they would and wouldn't do, and God help the tenderfoot who had the misfortune of gettin' tangled up with 'em. One time there was a fella come in lookin' for a job, kind of a tenderfoot, and that bunch jobbed him into standin' guard over the barn, said somebody was stealing' horses, and they give him this shotgun and loaded it with blank cartridges. And the foreman, he comes sneakin' in the barn and this fella was so scared he up and shot him. 'Course the foreman was in on the whole job, and he keels over and the boy goes runnin up to the house cryin' that he shot a fella. And the rest of 'em goes and wraps the foreman up in this old red quilt. Boy, the next mornin' when daylight hit, the tenderfoot had vacated."

Joe: "I think they used to do a lot more of that jobbin' than they ever think of anymore."

Mart: "Well, the men laid around more then, you see. There wasn't but a few top hands would get wages all winter and the rest of 'em would just get somethin' to eat. Some of 'em, you put 'em to doin' a little work, by gosh, they'd go on to the next place."

Dahl: "That old fella who used to be foreman for the Yankton about the time of the invasion, he had a crew up there in the pine ridge cuttin' timber. They had a dug-out up there, and he was a little leery of goin' around, so he told the boys in this timber crew, 'Now, any strangers come around or some of them Rustlers, just throw a coat over that limb on that tree to warn me.' Boy, he hadn't been any more than gone and they throwed a coat over that limb. He didn't show back up for three weeks. He'd ride in sight and take a look at that limb and (laughing) What was his name? They called him Kidney Foot. He didn't have a good thing to say about Rustlers. Thought they was all a pack of thieves and brand blotchers."

Mart: "They talked about blotched brands, but that was the petty thieves doin' that, what little of it that was done. And most of it they wasn't takin' off the big outfits, either. These big outfits had deep, definite brands, you know. The dry farmers just had these little bitty brands, and the petty thieves'd come along with big old brands and slap it on there and just blotch theirs all over it. I know some of it went through the meat markets here that you couldn't stop—it would look more like this fella's brand than anything, you couldn't tell **whose** it was. I saw that kind of thing up to about 1918, but it wasn't anywhere near what the cattlemen claimed it was. And most of the time it wasn't their stuff gettin' blotched. That was just another one of their excuses to start killin' men."

Dahl: "They wasn't all bad, though. Not all of them big fellas went along with the killin' and the invasion."

Mart: "No, that's true. Daddy Burnett always stuck up for the homesteaders. Made no bones about it."

Tom: "Did you ever hear the one about when Daddy's foreman caught a homesteader butcherin' one of Daddy's steers? And he come right in on Daddy at supper—and Daddy Burnett never talked business at the table. But this foreman thought what he knew was too good to keep, so he told Daddy about this homesteader and how they had a perfect case on him, take him right to jail. Daddy never faulted the homesteaders for eatin' beef, but this foreman didn't understand that. So Daddy says to him, 'Would you come over to the office after supper? I'd like to see you.' So the foreman went over, and Daddy give him his time. And the fella said, 'Well, what's the matter?" And Daddy said, 'I'm payin' you to look after the live ones, not the dead ones.'"

Mart: "Daddy was a pretty tough ol' rustler for being a big stock owner."

Pete: "One time I was with Daddy and he was talkin' about how he'd like to be a big cowman, and I said, 'Well, you **are** a big cowman, Daddy.' And he said, "Naw, I ain't big.' And I said, 'What in the world would you call big then?' And he says, 'To be a big cowman, you gotta owe a million dollars, and I'm only halfway there.'"

(Laughter)

Mart: "Ol' Daddy might've been a big cowman, but he sure didn't value money over people. He never went along with this greedy behavior. Then you had fellas like old man Waynes. He was a Civil War veteran, and he probably had around eighty, ninety thousand in appraisement on his outfit—and back then that was a lot of money. But as long as I can remember him, he had to get that $12.00-a-month pension. He'd even go to town to see about it. And at the same time, he might be losin' stock—cuz he never put out much hay. But he had to have that $12.00 whether or not he was losin' five or six head."

Dahl: "Don't that just beat all?"

Mart: "And I think of my mother, after father was killed, teachin' school and runnin' that hotel—she'd take in laundry to make ends meet when she had to. But, by the gods, she never took a dime from the government. We had it pretty tough goin', just Mama and us four kids, for a long time there. I remember once she got it into her head that she could save on the barber bill. Probably wouldn't cost two bits to get us kids barbered, you know. But she went and bought a pair of scissors. She got after us, and she thought some way or another that she should put the comb in there and cut **under** the comb. Boy, we had notches all over the place—worst lookin' kids you ever seen. Mama's probably the brightest woman alive, but she wasn't much of a barber. After the comb incident, she went downtown and got a pair of hand clippers. And they worked till we were growed and gone. But whenever we got a haircut, we just got clipped plumb down to skin. I was a great big kid before I ever grew any hair to speak of. She lost money on the scissors, but she sure saved on those clippers in the long run. She might not have been much of a barber, but Mama sure knew how to squeeze the last sigh out of a nickel."

Dahl: "Folks knew the value of money in them days."

Mart: "We sure never had much of it, but I don't ever remember thinkin' we were poor."

Dahl: "No, everbody was purty much settin' the same way, 'cept the big stock owners. And, by golly, I don't remember folks envyin' them their money, either."

Mart: "Well, they more or less gave money a bad name."

152

THE ROAN MAVERICK

Dahl: "Ol' Sol Braven sure hated 'em, didn't he. I think he was more of a wolf about it than Ben Lattis even."

Shorty: "He was quite a moonshiner, too."

Mart: "I heard a lot of stuff about him, but folks sure seemed to think he was alright. You never knew a nicer fella. He made the best moonshine whiskey in this country. When that other stuff was sellin' for $6.00, they come to Braven glad to pay $10.00. He had a good trade, but it was on account of his being clean. He was the neatest fella you ever saw. Fanatic on it."

Shorty: "Well, I was over there gatherin' horses at Braven's once. I didn't know he had a still, but he sprung it on me. He wanted me to go in with him, and I said, 'I may be broke, but I don't have to make a livin' that way. If I do, I'm gonna have to starve.'"

Mart: "The still was up Sulpher Draw, wasn't it?"

Shorty: "Yeah."

Mart: "The fella that turned him in was about the second worse double-crosser I've ever known. I wouldn't put his name out, but he turned the still in when I was sheriff and I turned it over to Owens while I had this appendicitis operation. Then the state and federal got into it, but they couldn't find any stills. So they come out and wanted Les Snow and me to take it over after I recovered, and course we had to do it. They had their papers lined up—warrants, you know. So Snow and I went out there. I told Braven I wanted to look around a little and he said, 'Go ahead.' He had a horse in the barn all saddled up and he let me use it. I was out a couple hours tryin' to track him around. See, he was workin' his still with pack outfits and horses without any shoes. Finally I guessed where he had the still. So I come back and said, 'I want to look over on that side a little bit.' There was a white-topped buggy in the yard with the top down, and Snow had been lookin' the yard over pretty good, and when he shook the wheel of that buggy, evidently he heard something gurgle. He reached in that top and pulled out a gallon of whiskey. He hollered at Braven, 'Is this good whiskey?' And Braven told him it was 120 proof, and Snow said, 'Come on over here and have a drink. You'll need it.' So Braven went and took a slug, and Snow had one too. It was already getting along toward evening, so I went down this draw and I happened to go up a little side draw and there was a limb had been broken off a pine tree. I went around this sharp bend and there was a still house that would hold fifty barrels. He had the still made on the order of one of these maple syrup outfits. And I looked in there and I commenced to get nervous, cuz I'd been told he was a shootin' moonshiner. Here was four barrels set up, lanterns under 'em, and I thought maybe I had better get ahold of Snow. He purposely stayed in the yard to watch our car. With it gettin' dark we was takin' a chance, because moonshiners would come in a tear up your car, run it over a bank or somethin'. So I got him and we had to work fast. We cut up the still and burnt the mash. There was plenty of kerosene, because they had a couple of these pressure tanks, and they were full. So we broke the tubing off and set it in under the door in two places where it would just shoot in there. It was a wonder we didn't blow ourselves up, because we forgot about them lanterns. When I thought of it, we threw an oiled gunnysack up against the door and really got away from there. Boy, that old still house just exploded. When we got out, nobody had bothered the car. But I talked to Braven and he said, 'I stood up on the side of the hill and watched you fellas burn that.' He thought I had found his horse track in there, and I never told him any different."

(Mart starts coughing)

Pete: *"Well, I went to the vet here the other day, but I ought to go see the Doctor once in awhile."*

Dahl: *"Who? The Chinaman?"*

Pete: *"Yeah."*

Dahl: *"Christ, if you wanna die, just pay me a little. I'll knock you off."*

Pete: *"Well, I reckon I got two chances with him in the neighborhood. If I can't get well through the Prodistant faith, I can have a go with the Buddhists. He's a good doctor, you know."*

Shorty: *"Mart, you remember the time you hired that cowboy from Arvada? He come by there lookin' for a job ridin' a rough string."*

Mart: *(coughing) "Kind of a light-complected fella?"*

Shorty: *"Yeah, big fella. And you told me that spring I could turn the rough string over. I had been ridin' 'em and was goin' to another outfit, and you said I could top me out a good string. You and myself and the girls corralled the cavvy, and we were gonna start towards Sussex to get the mail. And this fella come by and wanted to try some of these horses out that afternoon. You told me to cut 'em out for him, so I caught old Ape for the first one. And Ape, he'd stand, but once you stepped on him he'd hump up and run about fifty yards and just break in two, get to whippin' his head and strike, turn wildcat, you know. I'd rode him for a couple years, and the way I'd get by, I'd put a tie-down around his neck and just before he had time to break in two, I'd reach out, turn my reins loose, and I'd ride on that tie-down. He'd make three or four jumps and quit. But if you ever tightened up on them reins, he'd just turn wildcat."*

Mart: *"Wasn't there a mean little bay, too?"*

Shorty: *"Yeah, Torpedo we called him. He fell with me once and damn near killed me. But that Ape—this ol' boy was gonna try him out, and I told him, 'Don't pull the slack out of them reins, or he'll turn over with you.' So he led him outside the corral gate and stepped on him. Ape went out there about fifty yards, and the first thing this ol' boy does is set up on them reins, and Ape just turned wildcat. Mart, you was settin' out there on a horse and you roped Ape, brought him back, and this boy was gonna try him again. I told him, 'By golly, you better leave some slack in them reins or he'll turn over on you again.' And he went out there—done the **same** thing. Ape turned wildcat and lit right on top of him. Mashed him up pretty bad. So Mart caught Ape again, but this boy was gettin' a little scared then and wasn't so sure he wanted Ape. And I said, 'I'll swap you.' And he said, 'No, I'll try him again.' Stepped on him—did the **same** thing again. Ol' Ape caught him and just rolled all over him, darn near killed him that time. He didn't get up for awhile. Well, by then Mart was gettin' kinda sore, and he said, 'We might as well kill that horse.' And I said, 'No, I want him.' He was a good horse if you knew how to ride him."*

Mart: *"Pretty horse, wasn't he?"*

Shorty: *"Yeah, and he was a galloper, you know. A good circle horse—you couldn't ride him down."*

Mart: *"He was a pretty Appaloose. Had those streaks comin' down over his hips, and—"*

Shorty: *"But he was mean. He'd sure watch for the chance to kill you."*

Mart: *"Well, he didn't have but one brain cell."*

Dahl: *"Your Uncle Allison was quite a hand with horses, wasn't he?"*

Mart: *"Allison? Oh, yes, he had quite a string. He give me one of 'em when he left. And Mama give me his saddle and Winchester after we found out he was dead. She had 'em shipped down from Montana. Ally'd rope anything on anything, you know. Whenever anybody had really big stuff, that was Allison's work. And he wasn't a hand to get off a horse. He'd always get that horse around some way or another that he didn't get him jerked down. 'Course, he did that one time, and he was all broke up through the lungs. They were brandin' a bunch of big wild stuff and he got jerked down. The rest of those men—they were all top hands, you know—if maybe a runnin' horse come by or somthin', you'd throw out like that and catch that horse and step off 'cause your horse was gonna get jerked down."*

Dahl: *"But Allison would never leave a horse?"*

Mart: *"Oh, I guess he did sometimes, but he was awful hard to make leave a horse. And he was just as capable on a raw horse as on a good cow horse. He could work a round-up on pert'near anything."*

Dahl: *"He was a wild one, wasn't he?"*

Mart: *"Oh, he was always ropin' a wolf or chasin' bears into camp or somthin'—jobbin' somebody, you know. Joe, reach over and turn that thing off, and I'll tell a good story about Allison."*

CHAPTER ELEVEN
HOMESTEAD
(Excerpt form the Journal of Josie Watson Stewart)

*J*une 17, 1969 - *My great-granddaughter has brought me back to the homestead for the summer. At 107 I am too decrepit to be trusted alone anymore. Or so they think. Truth is, I wanted to come, and so did she. We wouldn't dare break our yearly tradition. By the prevailing standard of our family, she is an introvert. Quiet and reserved to the outward world, she owns a deep and subtle mind. I would say she is the logical hereditary conclusion of the Stewart/Watson clan. I can't say that I approve of the way my grandson, Tom, has treated her. When she was a baby, she was the apple of his eye, and he showed her off like a prize thoroughbred filly. But as she grew, he took her quietness for lackluster, and when she committed the absolute blasphemy of showing no interest in his constant stories of the cattle war, he discarded her like some ill-fitting shirt. It doesn't seem to faze him that she was graduated from the University with honors and is about to tackle a master's thesis. He is a stubborn man. I know why she chose the path of academics. She had to distance herself from the family history to fully appreciate it. One day she will outdo even him as the family historian, I just know it. And he'll probably be dead and have gone to his grave never knowing.*

Nothing pleases me more than standing on the porch of this old homestead, breathing the crisp air and watching Nature take her course around me. The valley is still remote, perhaps more so now than before. There are no Texas cowboys down yonder, and Whit's place has been empty for twenty years. The cattle are gone. I raise sheep, mainly because I still like to work wool. Spinning, knitting, weaving. But I can't get up on a horse at my age, so there isn't much point in raising hoof stock. The homestead doesn't amount to much but a summer retreat anymore.

I ran this place for decades after the children were grown and gone, stayed here alone until I was well into my nineties. Chopped my own wood, hauled my own water, and cared for the livestock. Martin put in a septic system in the late 1940s, and strung an electric wire up the valley for me before he was sent abed with the cancer. It was when he died in '53 that the grandchildren started after me about coming out of the valley to be in their care. I had spent so much time at their places while Mart was ailing that I was used to it by then. I agreed on the condition that I could still spend my summers here. My great-granddaughter, Angeline Watson Stewart, is the only person in the family who has taken the trouble to maintain that promise in the last fourteen years. I don't think the rest of them counted on my living quite so long.

When Angie started coming with me she wasn't more than eight or nine. At first, I think it was mostly done as a convenience for Tom—it provided a way for him to keep his promise to me while also allowing him to pursue his rodeos and occasional extra-marital flirtations. Much as I hate to admit it, Thomas Allison Stewart has mirrored the reputation of his namesake in more ways than being a cowboy deluxe.

We brought a television with us this time, a little twelve-inch affair—first one I have ever allowed across my threshold. But there is a special occasion forthcoming in July. One of these astronaut boys is going to walk on the moon, and I expect I had better see that.

Angie comes to me now in the half-light of evening, teapot and tape recorder in hand, an instrument one-tenth the size of that monstrosity Joe and Tom bought nearly twenty years ago. I seat myself in the rocking chair.

"Do you feel like talking?" she says.

"I haven't talked this much in eighty years, Angeline. I wonder at the brilliance of it."

She smiles. "Ever since I was a little girl, I've heard stories of the cattle war. Heard them told by four generations of cowboys. But you know what, Granda Josie? In all that time, I never heard one of those stories told by you, and I wanted to so desperately. You realize, of course, you're the only person left who actually lived it."

"That's part of the problem, child. Living it once was about more than I could take."

"I understand your reluctance. When Grandpa Mart was sick and they would turn on the recorder for all those oldtimers who came to visit, and they would start with their stories, you always managed to disappear without even a ripple—nobody even knew you slipped away but me."

"I had had a lot of practice at my disappearing act. By 1950 I had honed it to a fine art."

"Did you ever wonder why I always managed to find you?"

"No, Angel, I could see right off that you liked disappearing too."

"It was more than being shy around all those strangers. In some way I thought by following you I would be graced with the story no one had ever heard, that I was the special one you would share your wisdom with. Of course, I expected it to come in Aunt Joe's kitchen by 1952 while we were trussing a bird. I didn't think you'd make me wait this long."

"Well, look at it this way: You didn't have to waste much time finding a subject for your thesis."

She smiles. "Nobody's ever heard a woman's side of the cattle war."

"That's just about a contradiction in terms, Angie. The cattle war was a male outfit from start to finish. They didn't much care how women felt or whether they got tangled up in it."

"But it was as much a war waged on women as on men. Look at that unfortunate woman they lynched. And you, left a widow with four small children to raise single-handedly."

"Perhaps. But who's going to be interested in an old woman's story about range wars that happened in the last century? Don't you think this all might be a waste of time?"

"Examining greed and the abuse of power is always appropriate. If we don't question our worst behavior and attempt to decipher the lessons in our mistakes, how can we ever hope to correct them?" She's grinning at me now. "And if you truly thought your story was a waste of time, you wouldn't have spent the better part of a century writing that journal."

She's got me there.

"You know what I think, Granda? I think you have been waiting all these decades for the right moment."

"I think you're giving me credit for more discernment than I deserve. One thing I do think, though. I think I *was* waiting for you."

She smiles, fondly grips my hand, and turns on the recorder. "What do you miss most about the days of the beef bonanza—the days before the hostilities began?"

Jack, of course. I still miss him. And Will. I miss all of those men, and watching them work. Allison. Whit. Billy Shaw. All of them. Especially those Texans; they were really something to see. They roped differently than other cowboys, used a smaller loop— hardly any at all—just a little ring for the head of the steer. There was none of this flashy twirling a great big circle around forever and ever. They made a short swing and hit their mark, pure and simple. There's nothing nowadays that can compare. Oh, there are good hands now—I don't mean to disparage our present crop of cowboys. But it's so much different than it was then. Those men were tough, range-bred professionals. They couldn't jump in a pick-up truck and drive to town for a beer whenever they got thirsty. They lived on the range, and I really mean *lived* there. They knew every nook and coulie for a hundred miles. It was part of their job to know the land, and it also kept them alive. They were part and parcel of this earth, and that's something which is pretty much gone now.

And I miss seeing sights like the jerkline strings, the freight outfits with twelve teams, three wagons, and a cooster. They could haul twenty-five thousand pounds, and those wagons were heavy themselves. It was amazing to watch them out there on those crooked roads, with the jerkline horse controlling the others around the curves. I think Charlie Russell did a painting of one. There was a couple in this country, man and wife by the name of Roseberry, who had a freight business and each ran a jerkline outfit. They were amazing to see.

And I miss men with manners. It used to irk Mart to high heaven that these young fellas nowadays will wear a hat anywhere. Back then, a man took off his hat when he stepped indoors. Didn't matter who he was or if he was only going to be there a minute, he took that hat off his head. It would have been an insult otherwise. Now, it doesn't seem like these youngsters ever take off their hats. Likely they'll all be bald before they're thirty. Even at dances you see them wearing those hats, which would never have happened back then. No man would have been allowed into a dance with a hat on his head. Or liquor on his breath—they were strict to the point of religiousness about *that.* No drinking at a dance. On your way home was another story. If a cowboy was going to ride fifty miles to get back home, he might prime himself with a shot of whiskey to get going. But he never took a sip at that dance. And now—well, I'm just sorry to see that the use of alcohol has become so prevalent, among both men *and* women. Tobacco, too. It's a shame, because nothing good will come of it.

There are a lot of things I miss. It was a tougher life but simpler. And it seemed to be full of promise. People seemed to enjoy their work more. Perhaps it was the idea of a frontier that gave us that buoyancy. Of course, when you skin it right down to the fundamentals, it was an illusion. We were making our hope and prosperity out of someone else's misery, not unlike the cattlemen did to us. It wasn't *our* land, after all. The government had taken it from the Indians for our benefit. We never thought of it that way, of course, as making our happiness from another's misery. Perhaps that shows how ingrained racism is in our culture. We don't think of ourselves as racists, even though the fabric of our society, if scrutinized, would reveal startling evidence to the contrary.

But I miss the feeling that life was full to the top with opportunities. Of course, this was an illusion too. The sense of freedom and opportunity was only a pretty picture that hid a reality, which was dark and fraught with pain, as every injustice is.

"You've overcome oppression and tragedy in your life, Granda. Some say surmounting such horrors and tackling the journey of deliverance are the ingredients of enlightenment. Have you ever forgiven them? The cattlemen and Weston?"

I'm not sure their cloud had a silver lining, Angie. It was a dismal matter of overcoming the darkness, and I am not certain that is the same as enlightenment. Without the benefit of a conviction— or at least a trial—to vindicate the loss, the burden of retribution fell on the people. And in the absence of our right to lawfully assume the positions of judge, jury, and executioner, the burden of rage or forgiveness rested solely with the victims. I floated in a limbo somewhere between the two for half a century. Rage—Forgiveness. Long ago I managed to release my rage. On Jack's eightieth birthday, I stood on the porch of this old homestead and screamed at the top of my lungs, fury echoing off the red walls for hours as if the ghosts of my long dead cowboys had joined the terrible chorus.

Forgiveness often seemed like a one-sided transaction to me, an unearned absolution from the victim, available to anyone who commits immoral acts. But then it came to me after my good scream in the valley: forgiveness has nothing to do with absolving the criminal of his crime. It has everything to do with relieving oneself of the burden of being a victim—letting go of the pain and transforming oneself from victim to survivor.

And how can one absolve intelligent men for engaging in arrogant and demented folly? They knew better—every last one of them! Yet they allowed themselves to wallow in vanities, adrift on endless pretensions of grandeur, where the plotting of ever more grotesque absurdities became the norm. They were oblivious to reason and so deluded as to perceive themselves not only as invulnerable but as magnificently above the law. It was a blueprint for disaster, and even though we were its immediate victims, they could not escape its result either. They were the architects of their own fate as well as ours.

It was not surprising to me to find that many of the cattlemen most active in their decade of folly displayed in later years behavior oddly at variance with their tradition of self-aggrandizement, oppression, and greed. One returned to his small Pennsylvania hometown, never married, and lived the modest life of a dedicated philanthropist, bequeathing his entire estate to the Salvation Army and charities which champion the cause of the oppressed. One of the invaders, a Harvard man, had a nervous breakdown a few months after their capture and was sent home to the care of his wealthy family in New York. The leader of the group who lynched the woman homesteader and pre-empted her claim died a demented old man in a private Los Angeles institution. I suspect in all cases, once these men came to their senses and realized the lethal depth of their arrogance, their choices were limited to a driven attempt at atonement or permanent residence in lunacy. The question of whether I have forgiven them becomes insignificant in view of the historic magnitude of their folly. A more appropriate question would be: Could they ever forgive themselves?

Years ago when Mart was working the range, he happened to be on circle with Gil Herman's son, who—out of the blue—brought up the subject of the cattle war. He didn't know how his father could live with himself, he told Mart. He felt as if he had grown up under a dark cloud, and he was ashamed that his own father had ever dreamed of taking part in such organized and murderous insanity.

Part of the reason I maintained my silence for these eighty years was out of respect for the children, not just my own but those of the vigilante cattlemen and their hired guns. I knew Weston's daughters and Herman's children would have enough crosses to bear by mere hereditary proximity, and I had no desire to visit the sins of their fathers upon them.

For many decades, I thought the purpose of my life was to

reach the high plane of forgiveness, as defined by Christianity. But I was never able to convince myself that letting Weston and the cattlemen off the hook was the right thing to do. I was stuck in a misinterpretation. It took me all those years to learn the true nature of forgiveness. It's a deeply personal act, not of absolving the criminal but of self-absolution from suffering.

It wasn't until I launched my anger off these red walls and let it fly away into the night sky that I came to understand something that had eluded me my whole life. I may have looked graceful to others, but that was just a calculated suit of clothes I wore. Serenity would never be mine until I let go of the pain. Since that time I have come to believe that the purpose of life resides somewhere within a person's honest attempt to attain a true state of grace.

When I get there, I'll move on to greener pastures.

EPILOGUE

There is something else I miss: The smell of the grass and sage after a rain. Long ago I lost my ability to detect those subtle aromas. Once in awhile after a downpour I get the faintest whiff, so light its more like the memory of a smell than the thing itself. But even that is pleasing. It reminds me of Jack and our long-dead cowboys. I couldn't say why.

Perhaps it is because the range comes alive dressed in moisture. When dry, its colors are so subtle as to blend all together with only the vaguest hints of definition. It takes a good rain or a heavy wet snow to unlock its treasure of color—still subtle, but every hue enriched to its finest value so that each stands alone even while it pays shining tribute to its neighbor. The landscape becomes a painting by the most reverent and proficient of masters. If there is a God, this is his marriage with Mother Earth. Even though the aroma is only a memory, my eyes remain sharp and I can still *see* this artwork—the red willows a serrated slash of burgundy along the river, the gray-green-on-black of the sage, the reaching stems of the salt-sage, the cottonwoods, the red sandstone and granite, the endless stretch of grass a variegated sea of gold on green. I can almost see them riding there in the distance, my cowboys of the open range. It is my most prized possession, this painting. It's my reward for living and learning, for persevering through all the bad times—and my accolade from Mother Nature for paying her homage.

This beautiful Earth is what I will miss when I cross the Great Divide.